THE LEGEND OF THE SHEPHERD

IOANNIS NIGHT

Order this book online at www.trafford.com
or email orders@trafford.com

Most Trafford titles are also available at major online book retailers.

Printed in the United States of America.

ISBN: 978-1-4669-5906-4 (sc)
ISBN: 978-1-4669-5907-1 (hc)
ISBN: 978-1-4669-5908-8 (e)

Library of Congress Control Number: 2012917120

Trafford rev. 09/12/2012

 www.trafford.com

North America & international
toll-free: 1 888 232 4444 (USA & Canada)
phone: 250 383 6864 ♦ fax: 812 355 4082

"This is based on a true incident.
I can confirm it because,
I was present . . ."

CHAPTER ONE

MORNING

Two boys are walking inside an underground parking and straight ahead, the pathway leading to the upper floor. The parking was full of cars, each one in their attributed emplacement.

This is a huge parking as it was for the four buildings above. This complex comprises four buildings and all connected by this underground parking.

Hanged on a support pillar, is the red fire extinguisher which was placed here in case of fire.

The two boys are heading to an open green gate.

The first boy is nineteen years old and his name is Tony. He has an average body type with a shaved head. He has brown skin and he used to walk chin up. This day, Tony was wearing summer clothes and his mood was really good.

The second boy, who accompanied Tony, is of the same age. His name is Panos but his friends called him with a nickname. A name he got few years ago by a certain someone. Because he used to have a hunch like back at the age of fourteen, this certain someone started calling him "hunch man" or just "Hunch". Hunch has a fairer skin than Tony who is more in concordance with the rest of the people. This fairer skin made him look like a stranger in this own country. He did not really like to look than different and was trying to fit better among others working on this physical appearance. He got somehow a slimmer body but, he had only achieved to make it look even weirder than before. He was not fat neither slim. He was something in between but with wrong proportions.

Hunch's head had also his head shaved, not only because he likes the haircut, but as he admires Tony, he was taking him as an example to follow.

"It is annoying my friend, Hunch. Why is Nick always late?"

"He he . . . I don't know" he answered scattering his word as he was laughing.

"Stop laughing. You were also late! We were supposed to meet up at exactly nine o'clock." Tony stated with criticism.

"Yes, I am well aware of that but still, I am the first one to arrive even if it was not at nine o clock sharp!" he pointed his index finger as to make a point.

"First of the late ones . . ." Tony interjected gritting his teeth nervously.

As mentioned before, this parking was for the use of the resident of four buildings. Each buildings has two accesses to the parking underneath, one as the main entrance, the second was used for emergency.

Tony lives in one of the four buildings but not Hunch.

The pair was heading to a main entrance, the one from Tony's building, when a loud noise suddenly happened out from nowhere.

Someone was running towards them.

Tony stopped just before the entrance. He nodded at Hunch to do the same. A boy came out running and he seemed like someone was chasing him.

"Run! Run! He is coming!" he started shouting to Tony and Hunch as he pursued his race.

"Can you stop fooling around Nick? We have to go." Tony said with an annoyed voice.

Nick was making lots of noises, running in circle around them, screaming and laughing hysterically. After what he paused and stroke back.

"But it is true! There is someone coming after me! He was behind me, I saw him! Someone with a hole on his head!'". At the same moment from this same entrance, a tall bald boy appeared.

"Hahahaha! You meant Jim? Now I got it. A hole on his head . . . funny." Hunch laughed.

Nick was built and shaped as a professional athlete. He was a soccer player with a promising future and he had the style. He also enjoys making fun on people, including strangers, friends and even family members.

Nick was seventeen years old and he was tawny. The baldy one, Jim, was twenty four years old. He was the tallest of the four, and he already started showing the effect of alopecia. Probably for this reason, he started to shave this year as to hide the condition. To him, he was too young to lose his hair this way.

Tony didn't join in. He found the joke stupid and respected Jim above all.

Even though Tony liked having fun, most of the times, he was keeping serious, making jokes only when the situation was appropriated. This time was not.

Tony reached a red van and he started unlocking the door in the driver side.

The second thing he did, was to unlock the passengers door from the inside as well as the back sliding door. He ordered everyone to put their luggage at the back and to step in.

"I have an objection Mr. president! This boy here doesn't have hair, maybe it is contagious! I don't want to seat in the same car as him!" Nick requested making fun at Jim.

"Do you want me to beat you up now or later?" showing him his fist. Although it was a bad joke, Jim didn't seem to mind that much. They were all friends after all so they knew each other's reactions and weaknesses.

Tony sat in the driver's seat and he inserted the key on the starter. The engine began to roar. They were ready to depart.

They have planned that trip months ago but it is not until five days earlier than they started realizing that this trip could be one of the best time on their lives. They got organized for the trip and finally the time had come to live an experience all together. As they were all in their teen age, to be away from parents, only between boys, planning to act as they like, sounded like an ideal plan, on the way to paradise.

But it was only five days prior to the big day that they realized the importance of this trip. It was not only an excellent opportunity to have fun but it was as well the right time.

Good timing as they were young, innocent and excited to experiment the life of freedom. They were between friends, knowing each other from childhood and heading to freedom the time of the trip.

***** ***** ***** ***** ***** ***** ***** ***** *****

Golden summer morning. The light appeared when Tony activated the mechanical gate to open. The beams of the sun made their first steps into the garage.

It has been a relentlessly hot day. Jim stood from the window of the car, shaking his head, marveling at this exceptional weather. The sun was bright and the sky was clear. It may only was the ending of June, but in Greece the weather from May to September is crystal clear like this one.

Before they ride on the road as they were going out of the garage, Tony captured a familiar face crossing the street. Mr. Dimitris, 51-years-old professor, full time teacher of philosophy. A man they all knew, apart from Hunch, but they were all scared of.

In fact, he was not the most pleasant person in the world.

They waited for him to cross the street and they were also hoping that he had not noticed them.

All things set up, they were ready to take the road to their planned destination.

Tony's village was their destination and they had planned to stay for three or four days. His village was two hours away from Athens, their point of departure.

"And the trip began with Tony on the wheels!" Jim poetically said.

"And you are bald and the sun reflects on it!" Nick also poetically said to Jim, making fun at him.

"If I pour the juice that you are drinking on you then you will stop laughing!" Jim seriously answered to Nick's stupid joke.

Hunch was eating different kind of pastry snacks, from a box he was holding. He was sharing them with the others enjoying the idea of having a trip all together. Despite the fact that Tony had forbidden Hunch to eat inside his car, he did otherwise.

"Hunch! Are you stupid? Didn't I tell you to do not eat inside my car? I don't want you to make a mess and spread crumbs in my cleaned car." He yelled at him.

"And on top of it, I don't want you to eat them all. Should I remind you that your father gave that snack box for all of us to share!"

"I know. Have one if you like." Handing him the box.

"How am I supposed to eat it? Are you blind? Don't you see that I'm driving?" still yelling at him.

It was already not a long drive and done between friends makes it pleasant and always better than being on your own.

They were enjoying rock music from cd's they have burned especially for the road trip.

Because there was a bit of traffic, they assumed that it will take them a bit longer to arrive than they have planned.

All around them, the scenery was truly exceptional.

On one side of the road there were green plains and on the other side, there were big mountains covered with colorful trees of all kind. Only few kilometers away from Athens and the landscape was already astonishing.

They had nothing to be worried about. Four teenagers going on summer vacations, all together, is something that makes you feel utterly free and responsibility free. It was a good feeling.

Not that having a road trip was something new to them. They have done something similar by the past but they was accompanied by their parents. Not that they did not enjoyed it at the time but this time all parameters were different.

It was their first time, this gang, to be all together, away from parental supervision and allowed to be alone in country house, just there to enjoy every moment to the most and have fun.

There were still a bit of traffic jam but it was getting better so they could speed up a bit. They did not have any appointment so they were not in hurry but they wanted to get there and start the fun. The reason was simple: they wanted to spend as much time together as possible and to do not lose any minutes of it.

A car overtook them and Jim made fun of him saying that he was going so fast that soon he will meet with the reaper on the side road. The reaper was a character out of a scary movie who acts and killed road trippers.

Hunch started to say to Jim.

"Do you know about the legend of the shepherd?" He said mystically to him.

"The legend of the shepherd? What is that?" Jim started to wonder with excitement.

"You don't know about it?"

"No, tell me."

On his side, Tony looked at Hunch's face with a tiny smile.

"Well, Ioannis told me a story that happened thirty five years ago and his father was present. His father told him that one day, while he was coming back to the village from one of the surrounding town, he saw something strange . . ." Hunch wanted to say more but Tony cut him off.

"Hunch, man . . ." Tony said trying to speak clearly as he was eating one of the pastries.

Jim had given him to choose from the snack which he did but as he was also driving he could not hold it with his hand so filled his mouth with it. After he finally achieved to swallow the last piece of it, he used the back of his hand to wipe his mouth from any remaining crumbs around his mouth. Then he continued.

"Hunch, man, if you want to say a story you have to be more specific and give all the details." Tony was encouraging him to continue the story but giving some hints about how to make it more captivating.

"Ok . . ." Hunch replied and turned red as to apologize.

"So I will take it from now!" Tony decided to take over the story narrative from Hunch.

Tony and Ioannis are brothers and the story is about an event that happened to their father years ago. A story their father told them once when they were younger.

"Well my father once told me that when he was still living in the village, he was attending classes at a school outside. The village was small with only few stores and a church so he had to travel everyday by train to study in the near bigger city. Sometimes it happened that he took the night train because he had to stay longer there for unpredictable reasons.

That day, he took the night train and arrived to his village after midnight. Also in this small village, past midnight, lights are switched off leaving the road in the dark.

It is also worth to mention that back then the roads were not all equipped with lights anyway.

So, it was completely dark outside, my father could barely see where he was stepping. The wind was howling in a weird way. It sounded like the whistle of thousands ghosts flying around. The trees were bent by the strength of the wind which also made it hard for my father to walk against it.

Struggling to hold his coat closed against him, he felt like every step he was making was getting harder. Although the adverse circumstances, he had no choice, he was on his way home and there were no other way to make it.

The train station was on top of the mountain. Do you remember it? We have been there before. This old station, which is now abandoned, was working, on a daily basis forty years ago. It was the only connection between the village and the town. As the station was located on the mountain, my father as soon as he got off of the train, had to walk by foot to finish his journey and get home. It was a long walk, a walk he was doing every day and lasted about 20 minutes."

All in the car were listening to the story and impatient to know what happened next in the story. The story got the audience and they nodded when Tony mentioned the distance his father had to walk every day.

"Take it from now on Hunch. I show you the right way to tell a story." Tony gratifyingly gave him the right to continue.

Hunch was excited; he could finally be the narrator again.

"OK, so luckily for him, even with not much light to show him the way, the Moon was big and bright that night. As he made it down off the mountain, at some point even the wind stopped blowing but it got replace by a thick fog. It was not hard to walk anymore but with the fog, the vision got impaired and gives him this time a hard time to see. He could barely see.

Nevertheless, he did not really mind and knew that he will eventually make it to his house. Thus he was used to live under this weather. Those conditions were not really unusual to the region and in this period of the year. While he was walking, he suddenly saw someone coming out of the fog and quickly fainted away.

At first he thought that it was nothing and that it was just from his imagination.

But a blur image in the fog took shape.

In the middle of the night, nobody was out, not even the shepherds whose were numerous in the area. So he did not pay attention to it and kept walking. He was struggling to make his way home and all that mattered at that time what to be done with all that as fast as possible.

Out of the fog, a person appeared. It was a shepherd but he got no sheep with him. Not only that, this shepherd was wearing an old brown rotten hood on top of . . . . Nothing!! He did not have head!!" said Hunch with enthusiasm as the story turns more interesting.

"I don't get it." said Jim.

"Ioannis, and of course Tony's father as well, is a serious person. So I don't think that he could tell you a story of that kind. Your story is preposterous, it does not make sense. There are lots of inaccuracies as well!" He protested.

"First of all, I said that Ioannis told me the story and His father confessed it to him. Right, Tony? Your father have told you the story as well, haven't he?" looking in the direction of Tony.

"Yes . . . That's right." He dully answered.

"However, what do you mean by there are lots of inaccuracies?" Hunch asked Jim, impatient to know the answer.

"First of all, how do you know that he was a shepherd since he was not accompanied by sheep? I am sorry but that made me doubt. And secondly, he was beheaded? How was he wearing a hood then? You don't need to be a genius to figure that out. And anyway, what had happened after? Is that the whole story?" Jim started to lose his interest.

"No! I don't know all the details. I am just reporting you what their father had witnessed that night. I am sorry that I didn't finish my story. So, it got weirder as the shepherd disappeared as fast as he appeared. That is when their father froze in fear in front of that phenomenon. Standing still in stupefaction, the shepherd faded his way to the fog." Hunch said, completing the story for good this time.

"And you are expecting me now to believe that this is a true story?"

"I don't know. Their father would not make up a story just to scare me. He is a serious person with no interest on that kind of jokes" he blurted out. Jim didn't continue the pointless conversation. Even though he looked scared for a second, he didn't say anything more.

'Why do you say that their father did not want to scare you? Wasn't it Ioannis that told you the story? Will you decide and make up your mind?" Nick said, made a remarkable point.

"I have heard some parts of the story from the father himself but because he didn't really want to admit what had happened to him that night he did not go deeper in the narrative. So I asked Ioannis to tell me about that encounter and what exactly happened. Tony knows it all as well." Pointing at Tony, Hunch started protecting himself passing the attention on Tony.

***** ***** ***** ***** ***** ***** ***** ***** *****

They were going a lot faster now. The traffic jam was not surprisingly only in the suburb of Athens, now it was all cleared up and they were getting closer to the village. They were passing by a small town located near the village.

In this small town lived Tony's Auntie so they all decided to have a stopover to visit her and her son.

Tony had to slow down once more but this time it was because of some traffic works going on. The road had narrowed quite a lot, creating an alternated circulation. They were refreshing the road.

Jim started speculating about what they would do at their arrival. They were all excited. He also mentioned as a reminder that he has to talk to Ioanni as soon as he sees him. Nick had fallen asleep and ended on Hunch's legs. This late was trying to keep him up back straight without awaking him.

After they passed the road projects, they had to go through a long tunnel. Being inside the mountain and driving all the way through it was something that always fascinated Tony.

Inside the tunnel, there was not much traffic and Tony could drive smoothly and enjoy the traverse. Dark with only few road lightings, just enough to get a clear vision, Tony was relaxed and felt kind of light from his inside. Even though he had to be concentrated, not looking around, just watching the road, he was driving without stress and responded only by smiling or knocking his head.

At the end of the tunnel, the sun slowly took back its place, invading the entire surrounding environment with its bright sunshine. They got blinded from it for few seconds.

Nothing had changed with the weather. It was the same bright sunny day, a typical summer day in Greece.

They were getting closer to the Auntie's town now. Jim was chatting with Tony. They passed a traffic light, turned at the end of the road and found themselves at the doors of the town. They were now inside. A small Christian church in front of them, a garbage bin nearby, the streets were generally narrow in this area. Two cars would barely fit if crossing each other.

Jim got more and more excited. He was talking around all the time. This was not a disturbance for Nick who was apparently in deep sleep. Jim started to make fun at the sleepy head and the fact that he looked like he was dead. That made Hunch smiled but he got told off by Jim who criticized him because he smile like stupid all the time.

At some point, they had to wake up Nick. So Hunch started by shaking Nick's head in vain. He did it again, but this time harder. Nothing happened this time too. Hunch began to worry.

"Why isn't he wakening up? Do you think something happened to him?" bemused said.

Nick finally opened his eyes and with a fast movement, jumped from his seat, so sudden that he could have given Hunch a heart attack.

"Hahahaha. I enjoy this!" joyfully Nick said with the smile of satisfaction drawn on his face.

"Haha! You got me on this one." Hunch began to laugh and even though he had got pranked, he liked it. Everyone knew that Nick likes to make jokes and sometimes, his jokes could be of bad taste. Most of all, he likes to "play" with the poor Hunch who, by the way he was only, always been the perfect target for Nick's pranks.

Tony on the other hand, has a strong personality. That could have made him a defender for Hunch at the time but he wanted everyone to be united and considering that the jokes where part of their friendship life, he had never preventing them from happening.

He was still a student but he never liked studying. Opening books and spending time reading were not his cup of tea so he had chosen a different path, following his passion. Tony was into martial arts, he was training very often and he wanted to make it his future living and become a martial art teacher, running his own business, a personal dojo directed by him and in collaboration with some of his friends who also were into martial arts.

Nick was one of them. Soon he was training to become a professional soccer player. He would have finished school next year and could make it happen very soon. Everything regarding his personality shows up that he is a typical teenage school boy. Beside Nick and Tony, Hunch at the time and Jim, were not sporty.

Jim used to play volleyball, not professionally just as a hobby. He played with Ioanni because he likes it too and also because he was tall and a good volley player. They were playing for fun only and never came the thought of doing more than that. The volleyball court were located in their neighborhood and this two always manages to find enough players when all the conditions were reunited. Jim was also a student in a university and he was trying hard to finish it. He is easy going and fit with everyone, almost. Because he has one bad habit, he thought that he knew everything and he didn't like Hunch. Hunch was not really an enlighten person and so Jim had a grudge against him and slow people.

Nick pretended to be dead, but he kind of was at some extend as he is not used to wake up early in the morning. So after scaring Hunch to death, he eventually sit back properly and feel fast asleep again.

After a short driving inside the town, they finally arrived at the auntie's house. Tony was looking for somewhere to park the car. It didn't take him long to find a place right outside of the house, that street had been really been busy.

"We finally arrived at Tony's auntie's house?" Jim made a simple reference. He got off the car and walked few meters away from the car, and he noticed and pointed at a black chopper kind of motorbike which was parked close to their car.

"The only thing that we have to do now is to meet up with the others which, by the way, have ridden this motorbike." Jim told the others showing the bike.

Nick was still sleeping and he denied getting off the car. He wanted to sleep longer and did not care at all about anything else. He is a bit of a selfish person in general.

"Is he still sleeping? Come on Nick! I want to lock the car!" Tony shouted at him. But Nick didn't seem to care.

"It is the first person I have seen that sleeps literally standing up!" Jim commented.

The neighborhood was not bad, and the town itself was very picturesque. There are nice apartments and some of them have lovely private gardens. The buildings were not as tall as you can see in big city so the view was not masked and that make the town look prettier. A climbing vine was covering the wall giving on the parking and flowers were blossoming on every balcony making a beautiful and colorful laying decoration. They were of a maximum of three or four floors and they were not built as the apartments in Athens, here, you could see the sun, it was not hiding behind tall building blocks.

Still sleeping but also trying to walk, Nick did not another choice than to give it up to Tony. With his eyes half opened he got off the car after the second request made by Tony.

He and Hunch were following Tony. He was heading to the entrance of building where his auntie lived.

"It takes ages with you to go somewhere." Tony complained. Because they were taking their time until they walk. He rang the bell and a voice of a boy answered:

"Hello? Who is it?"

"It's me Void. Tony! Open to us." He commanded although in a familiar way.

A buzzing sound and the door opened.

They all got inside and after taking the lift till the fourth floor, the apartment's door was already wide opened waiting for them with Tony's cousin standing in front of it. Void was his nickname; almost everyone had a nickname in the gang. Sometimes they were also calling him the "cousin" due to the fact that he was in fact the cousin of the two brothers. But mainly his nick name was Void. He was a great student with excellent marks and he was always looking forward to experiencing new things. He welcomed them and offered them to come inside.

"Hello Void! How do you do?" Hunch jubilantly greeted.

"I am fine. And you?" he asked him in return, fixing his glasses up on his nose.

"He can't be fine. What is this for a question Void? Don't you see that shell on his back? Who could be ok having that thing on him?" this heavy voice was coming from the living room. Someone was lying on the sofa. Hunch laughed but with the small expression he had on his face, he showed that he was slightly annoyed from the bad joke. Even if he didn't like the joke, he preferred to keep it quiet and let it go. Void lowered his eyes, staring at the ground. He knew that when that person was around, he was always bad with Hunch but he didn't want to say anything. Void was the youngest among them, only fifteen years old.

There were two people sitting on the sofa.

The first person, from top to bottom was wearing black clothes and he had a beard and long hairs tied up high like a samurai.

The second person had brown curly very long hair and he was wearing a T-shirt with the name Nightwish stamped on it, from the well-known metal band.

The one who had talked to Hunch was the guy in black. His name was Ioannis and he was Tony's big brother, although, only one year separated them. He used to act

15

as the leader of the party, but after a recent traumatic breaking up with his girlfriend, he had no more the strength to lead.

Tony had turned to be the leader but Ioannis still had kept the respect. He was teasing them all the time when he had the chance to, but of course, his jokes could hurt someone and that was something he didn't know or he simple didn't care.

However, having lost his girlfriend and being emotionally unstable, his friends knew that he needed his time to recover. Making jokes against others was always his habit and him with Nick when cooperating, were making a real nightmare. But at the time, they weren't giving too much attention to what he was saying because they knew he was hurt and he needed to be active as a reaction to this bad experience of life.

He and Tony were practicing martial arts.

Next to him, Mr. Snake was sitting. This was another nickname given by Ioannis. But in contrary to Hunch, he liked it and not only that, he was also enjoying it. It was not difficult for Ioannis to name him like that since he was having a python as a pet on his house. Mr. Snake wasn't much of an athlete but he was doing sports as often as he had the chance.

From the school records, he was not a good student at all as he had failed on passing the exams last year, making him repeating the same class again. So, even thought he was eighteen and in Greece you have ended the school at this age, he was still in the last year.

Hunch went to sit opposite to them on another large sofa. The living room had four big sofas and a low table in the center. In the same room was the kitchen along with the dining room.

In one of the four sofas, Nick laid down after having his shoes off. The same thing Hunch was about to do as well but he had been interrupted by the Auntie who came to greet them so he did otherwise.

After all the necessary greetings have been done, Void started talking with Hunch in the living room and Jim who were installed in Void's room called Ioanni over.

"Come over here. We need to check your item on e-bay."

"That's right. I am coming now." He screamed to him because he was far and couldn't hear him clearly.

"You don't have any girls with you?" Auntie humorously asked Jim who for any special reasons was leaving the bedroom to go to the living room.

"No we don't have but he has long hair." he said and he grinned.

"Haha." The Auntie laughed softly.

"Why did you come here? I told you I was coming! Anyway, show me." Ioannis apathetically said to Jim. They went into the room and Tony was sitting on the desk on front of the computer.

After some seconds, silence invaded the space. The other followed in; they were all gathered in Void's bedroom.

It was a typical student bedroom. There were a library full of books, a single bed and a computer desk next to it, also a closet, nothing but an ordinary room.

"Do you have an e-bay account?" Void asked Jim who had taken over Tony's place in front of the computer. Jim didn't answer because Ioannis answered for him.

"Of course we have. How else you would be able to see an auction you think?" he said to him with a ruthless tone.

"You are all sick . . ." Tony whispered.

"E-bay is a life saver! Everyone knows that." Ioannis said as a statement.

"I would like to buy something too from here. I didn't know that you had an account. I always wanted to buy things I couldn't find in stores." Mr. Snake confessed.

In the background, Nick left the room and was trying to find the way to switch on the lights of the bathroom.

They had a small chat around an e-bay item that Jim wanted to buy and everyone was waiting for the results of the auction. After few minutes, the action was over and Jim had lost the item he was after. He seemed a bit disappointed but he forgot it all once Ioannis started talking about tonight's plans.

"We will watch the final of "Greek got talent" show and we will also make a barbeque tonight!"

"What exactly do you want to grill on the barbeque?" Tony who at the moment was sitting on Void's bed asked his brother.

"I don't know. Meat, I presume."

"I would say, shits!" Tony said. He was tired from the driving so got a bad temper.

"Hahahaha!" Hunch started laughing at Tony's answer but his laugh clogged instantaneously when Ioannis gave him a wild look.

"Are you enjoying it Hunch?" madly told him and softly touching his back. He didn't pursue the conversation, preferring to hide his smile and shrink on the chair as to disappear.

"We are going to have lunch here. Auntie invited us over for dinner, all of us." Tony added.

"Nice nice." Jim who seemed to like the idea said while Mr. Snake nodded vigorously.

"Jim, how long does it take to create a safe account online? I need to buy some items from e-bay." Mr. Snake asked.

"Only couple of minutes." He answered.

"Yes and you can use it the same day." Hunch also added wanting to show that he also knew how to do it.

Void left the room so Nick took the chance to pick up the toy axe which was on the desk.

He sat back on a desk chair next to Hunch and he began hitting him intermittently. He was targeting the hump, stupidly pretending to slice it up from Hunch's back. Ioannis started laughing so does Hunch.

"He hates him, he really hates him. I love this guy!" Ioannis cheered for Nick, giving him a friendly hit on the shoulder. Void entered in the room and Ioannis with a big smile on his face told him.

"You should be someone. You need to play someone else because your true self is nothing important."

"Yes I know. What do you say if I start saying all the time? Fay?" he beaming asked him.

"Fssss, Fssss." Mr. Snake started imitating the sound of the snake without reason.

"I don't know. Just do something different. I feel that you can worth more for your own life." Ioannis told Void who became sour about it.

"In each movie, someone has a role. You can be the nerd if you want, since you actually are one, but you need to show it more." Ioannis very seriously added.

Tony was at the veranda, he passed through the back door in the room which access to it.

The veranda was fully exposed to sunlight but Tony found a bit of shade and stood up there admiring the view. The air was heavy by the heat and it was unimaginable to go out and drive now, it was too hot and too bright.

"Sooooo" Nick started saying.

"What were you talking about during the trip, the three of you in the car?" he questioned.

"What?" Tony asked as he was coming back in.

"I heard something about a shepherd like a legend, am I mistaking?" he asked.

"You told about what had happened once to dad and what he had witnessed?" Ioannis continued questioning Tony.

"Your father had seen what?" Nick joined in showing his interest to know the story.

Hunch nodded and smiled again.

"They told me that their father had seen a shepherd one night, without a head. It was a quick apparition in the mist and it happened long ago when he was still a teenager."

Nick didn't say anything and Hunch started laughing secretly. He was thinking that the story was funny for some reason. He was not the kind of person to believe in supernatural phenomena. But later on, as soon as Nick lost his interest and stopped wanted to know more about it, Hunch followed, as usual, and he started believing that this story was nothing after all, just a waste of time.

"I can no longer see this face. He needs some serious slaps." Ioannis confidentially said to Mr. Snake, meaning Hunch's laughing face.

Running water from the sink in the kitchen was making a background sound. The auntie was doing the dishes washing plates and cutlery used for the breakfast.

Tony and Void was chatting about movies they have seen and they were exchanging their opinions.

"Ioanni, what is the website you used to download the full metal alchemist episodes?" Tony asked.

Ioannis didn't answer because he was too busy baptizing his friends with new nicknames. This was one of his favorite hobbies.

"Listen to that one! What about Hunch Man, the biggest victim of all times! Is it not a good one?" he said to Snake. The pair were laughing and enjoying it.

Those two were not close friends but since Ioannis travelled with him on motorbike and they got to spend more time together getting to know each other better. They had shared an experience, having done the trip together made them friendlier. So the baptism continued.

"Mr. Snake: a serpent with a long tongue, Jim: the gay, Tony: the irresponsible one who never stick to a time, always late and does not mind about it and my cousin Void who is of course . . ." Ioannis got cut off.

It was Nick. After the axe, he was now playing with a big mechanic insect toy and was acting like a stupid child.

Mr. Snake put a face and lay on the bed. He was the only one who though that Nick could be too juvenile sometimes and he could not stand it.

"Finally! He woke up!" Mr. Snake said reacting to the scene. Nick was so annoying to his eyes but Ioannis invited him and Nick was glad for that, so all that was worth it was the opinion of Ioannis, not Mr. Snake. Only Ioannis agreed to ask Nick to be part of the trip.

Nick was trying to make the insect fly around in Void's bedroom but It was a small room and the toy was not designed for it. He was dancing around weirdly, jumping about alternating legs. Not surprisingly, the insect fell down at each attempt and hitting everyone's head. That theatre made everyone, beside of Ioannis, upset and they started cursing him to stop the circus.

Indeed, all those cursing were not enough to make Nick stop as he had Ioanni's support. The both of them were laughing like crazy, acting like young kids that they were not anymore. That was their pleasure, to have fun, acting like carefree kids and also make fun of Hunch.

"Ioanni, do you think that we will need something else?" Jim asked in his attempt to stop the play.

"Do we have any masks? It would be funny to have some." He answered according to the situation not to the question. He did not have any will to stop the laugh that soon.

Nick continued to annoy Hunch who at some point could not take it any longer so he stood up from the bed and as he got upset, he shouted at Nick.

"Come on! I told you to stop it! That hurts!" He bawled out to Nick who had taken back the axe hitting him once more. Jim reacted and gave a handshake to Hunch as to congratulate him for counteracting against Nick and his stupid jokes. Jim was encouraging Hunch to proceed and made him feel victorious.

Until lunchtime stroked, Nick was teasing Hunch without break.

Hunch's bravery did not get any effect on Nick at all.

Tony wasn't paying attention, first of all because he was hungry and secondly because he was watching an anime episode online.

Even Void as owner of the place did not say a thing thought he didn't like it ever. This was unfair for Hunch but he didn't have the guts to cope. It was happening in his bedroom but he was the youngest of them all. He did not know Nick well enough to tell in off so he could not stand up for Hunch.

"And now, I will give the prize of the best hunch of this year to . . . !" Nick had the axe toy on one hand and a cup on the other one. He went towards Hunch.

"The best Hunch of the world!" Ioannis completed.

"TO OUR FRIEND HUNCH!" Nick grabbed him and tried to lift him up placing him around this neck.

Once again, Hunch got annoyed; he freed himself and nodded nervously showing his disagreement. He did not want the prize and refused it.

Ioannis looked at Nick wondering.

"He doesn't accept it?"

Nick's face turned red. He impulsively grabbed the small sword that Void had on his desk, souvenir from a trip to a Greek island, and pointed him with it.

"Take the medal you . . ." and viciously placed it on Hunch's throat.

What had saved Hunch from Nick's attack was the auntie. She called up as the food was ready, the table was set and they could start the meal.

***** ***** ***** ***** ***** ***** ***** ***** *****

Lunch was finally served. The table was covered with savory dishes and all seven like starving animals ate it all up. The auntie was filling up each ones plate but whoever had his plate served launched without waiting the end of the service. Even during lunch time, the bad jokes against Hunch maintained.

Ioannis made an admirable point about the way he was holding his fork. He had a theory about people and the way they are holding pencils and forks, as well as knifes and spoons.

This theory was that whoever holds his spoon with more than three fingers is believed to have brain abnormality.

Based on this theory, he enjoys making fun at slow minded people, people considered weaker than himself. Hunch noticed that they were staring at him because of that so he shifted the position of his finger and the way he was eating immediately because anyone could start a joke.

"Why are you changing it now Hunchback?" Nick ironically said to him. Everyone began to laugh with Nick. Hunch lowered his head and continued eating without paying attention to the jokes against him.

"I wish I had a chainsaw" Nick mumbled thinking of cutting off Hunch's hands.

The jokes are part of the lunch and most of them towards Hunch. They emptied their plates and all dishes that were in the center of the table. They also had eaten in the car lots of pastry snacks from Hunch's father but at that age it is not surprising to see them eating so much.

Tony was telling a story about someone they all knew and the way he was threating girls. He also mentioned that the girl in the story was finding Hunch more attractive than Jim, astonishingly.

She confessed to Tony that she found that Jim also had a hunch on his back and that he was way uglier than Hunch. Jim knew that this girl hated him because he didn't like her at first but Hunch, when he heard that statement made from a girl who appreciated him more than one of his friends, he jumped up and he run towards Ioanni.

Ioannis had left the table once done with his lunch. Therefore he was lying on the sofa listening to the story. Hunch loved him as friend, even if he was not threating him well sometimes and extensively making fun at him. Hunch grabbed the opportunity to approach Ioannis and start to make fun at Jim. For once, he will not be the victim but the tyrant.

They both laughed on Jim's hunch this time which they agreed to see. For the first time since the trip started, Hunch was enjoying the moment and he felt like he was having some fun.

Void after eating his lunch, stood up and filled a small bag with clothes. He was packing as to join the group on the trip. Jim advised him to take more stuff but he denied for the reason that the village was no more than fifteen minutes away from his house. Therefore, if needed, he could easily come back to pick up more things.

They gathered their belongings from Void's bedroom said goodbye to the auntie and off they went.

This afternoon was hot and hazy and only one small cloud could be spotted.

For this journey, Nick wanted to ride the bike behind Ioannis. Without any objections, the exchange was made.

Mr. Snake and Void got aboard the big red van. Tony ordered them to take a seat at the back and he switched on the CD player. The engine was roaring so they were finally ready to depart for the coveted village.

***** ***** ***** ***** ***** ***** ***** ***** *****

"Here we are!" Ioannis posted. They finally arrived at destination.

Void had the keys of the house. Tony had handed them to him while he was helping to load the car with the luggage. Void holding the car key with one hand; he went to unlock the house gate with the other hand. All the others were coming one after the other charging the boot of the car. Void could not open the gate.

"This is weird." He muffled.

"The alien comes, give a way!" Nick passed by with the helmet on his head.

"Let me give it a try." and he tried to open after snatching the keys from Void but, failed dramatically.

"The door may be cursed!!!" Ioannis spookily said wiggling his fingers.

"It's an old gate and most probably there is something wrong with the keyhole. This not surprising that I cannot unlock it . . ." Nick soundlessly said not wanting to admit that he could not open it.

"We have not got anywhere yet and already weird things happened." Ioannis added intensely.

Hunch was the last one coming. He had taken only few things with him for the trip: a small blue travel bag and a plastic bag with only few extra things. The plan was to stay more than two days and Jim previously warned him in the car that that would not be enough for the whole trip. On the positive side of it, he was travelling light comparing to the others which was an advantage when you have to carry it around.

"I will give it another shot." Nick pushed it harder this time and finally the door opened.

"As I said, it only needed a bit of hard twist." Nick proudly alleged.

Behind the door, there was a yard, no bigger than fifty square meters. The ground was damaged by the time and became as asymmetric here and there. It was not perfectly flat and there were three small steps badly built and leading to the front house door.

Nick shrieked and by his body position you could see that he got scared of something.

"A butterfly!" he said.

This joke was a success one as he got all the audience and everyone laughed. But again, before he opens wide, he stopped.

"What again?" Mr. Snake asked him who was just behind him.

"I am not going inside. I think that there could be thieves in there!" he stated refusing to go any further. Tony pushed Mr. Snake away, passed Nick as well and he entered in first.

"Thief, thief, are you in there?" He melodically sang.

"Yes, there is one here . . . dead from . . . ." Mr. Snake wanted to keep going but Tony caught him first.

". . . dead from the terrible musty smell." And he started laughing.

The house contains five rooms. Two were bedrooms, one was the kitchen and the largest one was the living room. In the living room, the family has disposed three convertible sofas. Therefore this house was a perfect holiday house as it can host many guests at the time.

Passing the door, you get to the veranda with three other doors. One was to a bedroom, another one was leading to the corridor of the house and the third one was the toilet.

The master bedroom had two exits, one to the corridor, the other one to the living room.

Slowly, one by one, they got inside the house. When all in, the first thing they saw was terrifying.

"Oh! A scorpion!" Mr. Snake said out loud.

"OH my God! Kill it. Do it fast." Nick started shrieking but this time it was not part of a joke.

"No do not kill it!" Mr. Snake loudly provoked Nick from doing something unfixable. Mr. Snake was a fond of creepy insect like snakes and scorpions; he used to have some as pets. So there were no valuable reasons to his eyes to kill the scorpion standing in front of them.

"Yes I strongly agree. We will not kill it." Tony joined in Mr. Snake.

"Are you stupid? It is going to deadly bite us all." Muzzy Nick said.

"Another bad sign . . ." Ioannis muffled but Jim heard him.

"I believe too that this is a bad sign. Since the beginning you are telling me about that story with the shepherd and now this and before we had the door." Jim said with a slight of anxiousness on his voice.

They were staring at it and after few seconds have passed, they eventually decided to kill it. They didn't want it to come again in the house if they were just moving it outside. So Tony took a napkin and threw it, covering it totally. Then Hunch stepped on it and with his right leg, it finished it.

"It was a bad sign that the scorpion was here . . ." Nick said probing. Jim shook his head, confirming Nick's words.

"Hunch, now that you killed it, I strongly recommend you to eat it and tell us if it is tasty." Nick derisive said and he decided to stay on the small bedroom which was the first room he saw.

As the event with the scorpion had finished, everyone had started searching the house. Looking for a place to leave their luggage and decide where to sleep.

Nick at the moment, was alone in the small bedroom and he instantly saw something that took the soul out of him.

A giant bee was flying in all over the room. Nick when it saw it could not believe his eyes. He was not really afraid of bees, but the size of this one could easily scare anyone.

He did some steps behind and with the edge of his eye, he saw another weird thing happening. A black cat outside in the yard, staring at him. All this time, he was carrying on his back an electric guitar. He left sluggishly the room and he left the guitar in the door of the room. Then he yelled so everyone to hear.

"A scorpion a black cat and a giant bee! We are all going to die!"

"This is a bad omen, sure . . ." Ioannis mumbled making fun on him.

Tony was putting food on the fridge while Void is trying to understand why Nick was making all this fuzz.

"Black cats . . . scorpions . . . I know whose fault is that! Is yours!" Jim critically pointed at Hunch, who as always replied with an innocent smile.

"This is all is entire your fault and do not smile. This is your first time here and already we have seen a black cat, a giant bee and a scorpion. This is a warning!" and heated he accused him again.

"Let him be. Let's decide where you should sleep now." Ioannis told Jim.

Jim had decided that he would be sleeping with Tony and Mr. Snake on the living room. Ioannis and Void had already taken the big bedroom, which had two beds on it, and Nick with Hunch, would be sleeping together in the small bedroom. One on the bed, the other on the sofa.

They didn't want Nick to sleep with them because they knew he will do pranks if he had the chance, so at least, having him away from them was safer.

At last, Ioannis was in his bedroom, taking things off the luggage and placing them in the drawers. In his peace, doing something as simple as ordering the clothes, a breaking sound took him out of his calm sphere. Something from outside. Something had broken.

He did aside the curtain of the window to see and with big surprise the shutter of this window was broken.

"Oh! Guys, the shutter broke by itself without reason!" he could not believe what had just happened.

"Hunch broke it!" Jim categorically but with a funny tone on his voice said and pointed him.

"Hunch! Please be serious, do not break other people shutters." Ioannis anxiously but knowing that he had nothing to do with it, blamed him.

"I did not do anything . . . I was standing here, how could I break it?" he wanted to protect himself but Ioannis did not even care about his statement. He left to the other bedroom and he enthusiastically said to Nick, who after taking the bee out of the house, was playing with the electric guitar.

"The shutter broke by itself! Can you believe it?"

"Listen this one; I am playing it very nicely!" Nick concentrated to the song answered him.

Ioannis stayed with his mouth opened but no sooner than he realized that no one was caring about the incident, he continued with the unpacking.

Maybe, because they haven't heard it, they thought that it was another of Ioannis jokes so they didn't give too much attention. Once he saw that they didn't care for that, he through that it could be a rational explanation for that and he didn't come further with that.

Especially he, couldn't care less for things alike, so he took off the luggage the rest of the clothes and personal stuffs and first thing to do after that, was to charge his mobile.

The problem this time was that he could not find his mobile.

He went on the living room and started asking if anyone has seen it. Jim and Mr. Snake were playing with the x-box there and they were completely absorbed.

"Someone stole it." Jim said without even looking at Ioanni.

Ioannis knew that they were not much of a help. It was his mobile that was missing and not theirs, so they were acting like nothing was going on.

Hunch was in the same bedroom as Nick and he asked him if he had forgotten it somewhere.

"Of course I haven't! I simple lost it!" Pissed off responded to Hunch. The only person who had always things under control was Ioannis and now, he had something going on and he could not stand the fact he may have done a mistake such crucial as losing his mobile.

Moving from one room to the other, looking madly for it.

"Why do you care so much? It is just a mobile." Mr. Snake careless told him. They were still p[laying with the game and for this reason, they had no connection with reality. It was like they were brain washed. Eyes pinned on the screen.

"I can call you so as you, hear the ringtone and find it!" Jim yelled on him from the living room as Ioannis was looking for it in his bedroom. But he did not answer. He relaxed and said to himself.

"Whatever, doesn't matter, I will find it sooner or later."

Void and Tony, had finished unpacking their luggage and now they were preparing to relax as everyone else was already doing.

The day kept going as it should be.

The guys, who all apart Ioanni liked football, had their attention at the x-box matches. They also made a tournament to compete with each other.

Tony had brought along his netbook and he was watching a movie. Nick joined him as well. They wanted to do as many non-active activities as possible. This was their plan from the beginning and they were enjoying it at the maximum.

A card game as well was part of the day's cool down program. Void and Ioannis were the ones who liked card games and they could play for hours if they had nothing important to do.

Games were the base for a perfect summer lessening trip. Jokes against Hunch taken place times to times but Hunch was also participating in jokes against others. They were having great time and even though they were slightly tired from the trip, they didn't want to rest by sleeping.

Mr. Snake only tried to do it but they were all making so much noise which was impossible for someone to sleep even if he wanted to.

As the day continued, Nick and Hunch decided to go and play basketball in the village's kinder garden.

It was an open area which had two baskets, not the size of a stadium though, but this was enough for the two friends who tired by playing computer games wanted to do something different.

For Nick who was an athlete, staying inactive that long was already intolerable. Hunch wanted to improve his body abilities and gladly volunteered to go with him. Is about when they left that Ioannis began saying the story of the shepherd to Void.

"Have you ever heard of the story of the shepherd cousin?" drilled asked.

"I do not know . . . I thought that it was just a story you came up with." And blinked once his eyes.

"No, not at all. It really happened." Ensured him.

"I do not know. You told me I think but to be honest I don't believe it anyway."

"My father had seen it. You can call him if you don't believe me." Peacefully throw down the gauntlet on him.

"Ok, ok. I know what have happened. I do not need a reminder." Void tried to avoid Ioanni repeating the story. He actually knew it and had no mood hearing it again.

Ioannis smiled at him and he gathered his deck on a box, he left. Went out to walk, give some time to him, to relax, alone . . .

. . . away from everyone's presence.

CHAPTER TWO

EVENING

On summer time, night falls around nine o' clock in Greece. It was evening now and the sun had not dusk yet.

Everyone because of the heat had their shirt off. They were all sweaty and they were walking around the house and the yard half naked. Men's mind doesn't care about nudity, especially when it is only men around.

They all had gone after Nick and Hunch few minutes later. Having a great basketball game, competing even there against each other, their body temperature had risen significantly.

Fifteen or so minutes now that they had returned to the house, waiting their number to go and have a shower. There was a problem with the heater and they had to use hot water only once per day. Tony had strictly instructions from his father so he left no one to use hot water twice.

This of course was not a problem as it was summer and they were not that much using the heated water.

As it was meant to be, Ioannis was the first one to have the shower. He had seen them from the mountain when they were heading to the basketball field and he joined had them in an instant. Pretty much, everyone had his shower and it was only Nick and Hunch who hadn't done it yet.

Nick was already in the shower and he was singing loudly.

Hunch after the game was extremely weary. He was having a pathetic look on his face. Even the jokes could not affect him at this point. Mr. Snake passed in front of him, walking out on the yard.

"Nice weather isn't it?" he asked Ioanni.

"Nice belly you have there, isn't it?" responded with irony.

"Screw you." Mr. Snake answered and gifted him a sinister smile.

"Hunch, what about your body? Will you reveal this absolute goddess shape to us?" tone still ironic.

Hunch ignored him and lowered his head with his eyes on the ground, avoiding Ioannis mood for jokes.

As Mr. Snake had mentioned, the weather was in its best right now. The heat had been reduced as the sun was hiding behind the mountains every minute and the sky had this amazing orange color. Could not be missing in this great day the singing of the birds of course. The harmony of Mother Nature had put her spells on the seven friends.

This was it, the perfect summer vocationally day they were looking for.

"ts ts ah ah ah . . . . Ts ts ah aha ha ha ah . . ." This was a noise Jim made to look similar to the soundtrack of Friday the thirteen. A classic horror movie.

All of them adore horror movies and they were watching them with passion. But among them, Ioannis and Jim were the ones who had watched the most and they were calling themselves "experts".

The singing coming from the bathroom was not pleasant. Nick was singing aggravating and as loud as he could. Ioannis went close and cursed him but he only made things worse. He was taking his time, enjoying the bath and enjoying the noise he was causing.

"I am going to show this boy what means to mess with the MASTER' meaning him. He went to the yard and there was a small window, closed, but it was there. This window was the bathroom. Ioannis went under it and talked to Nick.

***** ***** ***** ***** ***** ***** ***** ***** *****

In Greek language, male's first names are all having the suffix "s". When someone is introducing his name, he puts the "s" on it. Also, when someone is referring to a person, again the "s" takes place. But you do not put the "s" when you are talking to that person. You just pronounce the name without the "s".

***** ***** ***** ***** ***** ***** ***** ***** *****

"Have you seen my mobile? I am seriously looking for it now and it's nowhere to be found." This was not his first though when he went there but he remembered he had to find his missing mobile too.

"No my friend. Haven't seen it. Do you want me to sing you something?" Nick humorously asked him.

"No . . . No one has seen it. This is getting weird." Ioannis stated and left.

Mr. Snake unzipped a small bag he had with him and he began searching the pockets one by one, eagerly. Jim saw him and asked why he was panicked.

"Because someone is stealing mobiles. That is why!" Kind pissed off said.

"What?" He laughed without believing him actually.

"I cannot find my mobile too." Mr. Snake specified with his words that his mobile had gone. Some mixed feelings wormed their way back. Losing one's mobile is justified, two, means something is odd.

"Mine is missing since we arrived here remember? I was searching for it to plug it on the socket and could not find it." Ioannis not so much worried added. He had started to believe that he could have probably left it at his auntie house and there was no need to rush his anxiety with it.

After all, there is always a reasonable explanation for everything.

But still he did not like the fact he wasn't having it with him.

"I think I left my mobile back home." Void murmured.

"What? You do not have it as well?" Hunch who was next to him amazed enquired. On his face, you could not see negative feelings but excitement and deeply satisfaction.

He was the one who was always behind, doing mistakes, blamed for everything, an extra man, an extra weight. Now seeing this, everyone forgotten their mobiles, he was feeling superior. Could not hide his true feelings which were not other than pleasure at the moment. Once he was not the one who had done something stupid and as it was natural, he was kind of enjoying. Unfortunately he could not conceive the extension of the problem.

They were three mobiles off and that was a fact now.

"Did you take it Hunch?" Mr. Snake gave him a wild look seeing his face smiling.

As he heard those words, his face turned pale. A big question mark appeared over his head. Could it be that they were really accusing him? First time he was on top of them and still, they could make it seem like he did it?

Or he had really something to do with it?

"No!" Hunch replied, his tone concerned as he had been accused for murder.

Jim offered to help find the mobiles in case they were still in the house. He searched under beds and sofas for short but he found nothing. Mr. Snake was trying to remember if he had left it somewhere else as Ioannis acted certain for having forgotten it in the auntie's.

On the other hand, Hunch wasn't sure what Ioannis was trying to do. His easy going comment about having forgotten it back in the town was elliptic. He had seen him taken it with you from the house.

Even though, Hunch was acting weird and it was not hard to notice. Something was going on here and answers should be given fast.

"Hunch! Come with me outside for a minute." Jim told him. He went out in the yard and Void followed as well. Jim was eating something and with him mouth still load announced.

"I have lost my mobile but I know who is behind that prank." Jim words were more argumentative, more loaded with hate as usually, his tone oddly harsh.

"Who?!" Void said looking socked.

"Hunch!" he testified and he seemed a hundred percent certain for his answer. Hunch shook his head and left the room, having an expression of disappointment.

"I am two hundred percent certain that I have left it on my auntie's." Ioannis opened the door, said, and went back in but still remaining in the entrance hall.

"I suggest us all to take axes and fix his hunch!" Nick yelled from the kitchen, hearing Jim's charges.

"It was, the last time I saw it was on my desk with your keys." Void reminded Ioanni.

"IOANNI!" Hunch called from the TV-bedroom.

"What does he wants now?" he thought and went to him.

"I have to tell you that I did not touch the mobiles." Said through his guarding words.

Ioannis took the opportunity to look into his bag, wondering if he may have something to do with it.

There was nothing. Not there at least.

Half naked lying on the bed, Mr. Snake with only wearing his boxer, was asking if they were trying to make him worry by taking his mobile. Ioannis told him that, at least he had nothing to do with it.

"I still insist! Axes are the only way!" Nick kept saying, yelling from the kitchen while he was having a sweet meal.

"What does it have to do with the fact that we all lost our mobiles?" Ioannis neutral asked Nick. But Nick without restrains started laughing hysterically and loud.

Again as annoying as he could be.

"Guys guys, listen." Jim called everyone to join them on the yard.

"I have to tell you . . ." Hunch did to say but Jim did not let him.

"Listen, you said it yourself. I had left my mobile there, on the stone hedge around the yard and you told me that no one has gone there all this time and you were the only one around here. Right?" Jim tested him. Hunch did a marveling expression and Jim continued with his charges.

The yard was protecting by a stone wall, not too high. Jim after the game, he had left his mobiles in the edge of the wall for a better reception. Hunch had seen him putting it there.

"So, if you were here all this time and no one had taken it, then who should I suspect?" also, after he left it there, Hunch was around the yard all this time, getting fresh mountain air.

Hunch began having a small awkward laugh. He did not know what to say, since he indeed was there the entire time. However, he took a breath and he tried to explain himself.

"You have to believe me. I did not take it!" and the awkward sense from before was mounting.

"You want to make a joke and even that you cannot do it right!" accusation from Jim's side going on.

"Grand Victim!" a voice from Ioanni's mouth sparkling said.

"An epic idiot I would say better. How do you insist that you have nothing to do? How? You were alone here! The mobile didn't jump out of the house alone!" his tone more critical than ever.

"I am not joking . . . I didn't take it. I know how it sounds but I didn't." Hunch justified.

"This boy here is Jim. Twenty four years old studding electrician." Ioannis started giving them ranks.

"Your mobile Ioanni is on my desk, I remember it." Void told him.

"I am not lying1 I didn't take it" Hunch after Ioannis having finished said, while Void was saying about the mobile.

"Yes ok . . ." Jim shook his hand and turned his back on him.

"HE DOESN'T BELIEVE ME!" shocked addressed to the others.

"Twenty years old. Student on the public school of telecommunications. Zero skills, zero abilities, minus zero intelligent." The ranking was going fluently.

Mr. Snake having dressed after the shower joined the team.

"Mr. Snake, eighteen years old. Still a student as he had failed last year to pass the class." And a tiny smile appeared on his lips.

Mr. Snake nodded meaningful; he really could not care less about school. Ioannis wanted to make a ranking criteria for everyone without any particular reason. He walked inside the house and found his brother, Nick and Void and gave them some random, bad, ranks as he have done with everyone else. Only for him said great words, full of brilliantness and once he finished, went outside, but only for a second.

"Your breath stings." His face close to Hunch's; the late afternoon light enchanted it. The door closed behind him, walking back in. Everyone else did the same, leaving Hunch all alone.

He was sad, not because the way they were treating him, he was more or less used on that. It was more because he could not accept the unfair charges on his name. He wanted to laugh and cry at the same time. Mysterious feelings were coming to the surface. He was never doing anything wrong and still, after all these years, they were putting the blame on him. Chatting with himself, serious happenings adjoining them and they were not focusing on the real problem. The scapegoat was his role in all this. They have lost their mobiles and they needed someone to put the blame on. He knew he have not taken them but he also knew he had no proofs that he hadn't.

The sun's hard core light from the morning fainted as the sun all the more was hiding behind the mountains.

There was definitely something going on. If had not taken the mobiles, then who?

***** ***** ***** ***** ***** ***** ***** ***** *****

Void had started feeling unease because he could not find his mobile. He was squeezing his brain to remember if there was something he was forgetting. Was it here or had he left it on his house? Hunch was near him, watching him straggling with the thoughts: had he lost it? Had someone taken it? Or simple he had never taken it with him?

"All of the mobiles are gone now?" Hunch comprehended asked him.

"Yes." Void clearly nervous answered.

"There is no reason to be nervous. Someone has just taken it and he will return them sooner or later. Calm down." Ioannis who was nearby answered him seeing pretty sure about his answer.

"Even that phone here . . . the landline doesn't work." Void swallowed his words.

"What?" Jim emerged and tried it out.

"Maybe the signal gone." Ioannis suspected.

"But before it was ringing! Believe me, I tried it when we arrive here." Void with his worried tone told him.

Hunch observing everything, changed his sadly face into a smiley one. If the landline was not working then he had nothing to do with it. He was off charges. The feeling of being clear gave him the courage to breathe again normally.

Mr. Snake was playing alone with the console. Hunch sat next to him.

"It's amazing. Nothing is working!" and a big mouth opened smiling.

"I don't understand why it is not working!!!!" Void was shouting and running upside down apprehensively.

"Calm down!" Ioannis gripped him from the shoulders, trying to bring him back to his calm self.

Jim was trying to do something with the phone but with no result.

"In half an hour or so, Greece got talent will begin. Let us all lie down and watch it without worries." This was the main event of the night and Ioannis did not have any intention to lose it. He wanted everyone to relax and join him. He was planning this night for a month now and he wanted nothing to go wrong.

But Hunch could not relax so freely.

"You have something to do with that! And the missing mobiles!!!" turned his finger pointing him.

Hunch who was relieved one second ago could not believe in his ears. He was still the one to put the blame on?

"What did I do?!" he yelled and his feelings overtook him. He left the living room, walking out of the house.

Jim was still accusing him for everything, it was unbelievable. There was no way he could accept it.

Unpremeditatedly, Void picked the phone of the house to double check. What he heard left him fearful. The phone rank once and then . . . dead. Hunch saw his expression as passing to go out and his hairs all over his body chilled.

"What?" Hunch with an alarmed tone asked.

"The phone . . . The phone rank once and not doesn't work again . . . ." Void said and left the stony earpiece on the table.

"Really?" Jim was studying to become electrician and it seemed weird what Void said about ranking only once. He had one more look. He pressed the phone button several times just to verify if it was not working.

It did not.

"We do not have phone . . ." This was Ioannis final statement.

"But this cannot be happening. It was ringing before and it rank now!" Void openly panicked said.

"Maybe the lines, because we are on the mountain, have gone down. I told you already. As for the rank, it is still a machine, sometimes they do their own. There is no reason to lose your temper cousin." Ioannis once more tried to calm him down.

He was getting panicked easily. After all he was only fifteen years old and still addicted to his mother.

"But we do not have phone. This doesn't work at all." Jim said with query on Ioannis unbiased reaction.

"What is happening with the telecommunications?!" Hunch having a huge smile on his face added.

The smile was only for one reason painted on his face. Excitement! Even if they were having no phones, this exhilaration was coming out of unexplained.

When something mysterious and out of the ordinary line happens, then people sometimes get excited no matter what is happening. This was the case now. Hunch knew that something was wrong but he could not hide his enthusiasm before an unnatural episode.

"YOU ARE THE ONE STUDYING TELECOMMUNICATIONS! FOR ONCE OPEN THAT SELL ON YOUR BACK, TAKE OUT SOMETHING USEFOUL LIKE THE SUPER MARIO AND HELP US!" Ioannis funnily but shouting said to Hunch.

"But I was able to call before. It hasn't been a while since I tried it . . . it is amazing." Voids, face wondering around on the air, looking for potential answers.

"Never mind. Soon we will have it back. It is not like it is happening for a first time." Ioannis said this as an answer to his cousin and followed Hunch. He was still excited for what was happening but the incident with the phone reminded him an unfinished business. He was still the one Jim blaming for the loss of his mobile and most luckily everyone else's.

"I have to find it at any cost!" He was looking motivated everywhere for Jim's mobile. It could not have just disappeared from alone. No one else was around there at this time and the mobile had not fallen on the other side of the wall where the road was.

It was a true mystery. A way bigger mystery than the landline phone. He was being blamed and he could understand why Jim was blaming him.

The blood on his head had raised and its face was red.

"Will you forget already about that?" Ioannis gently asked him, pushing him in a way to quit.

"No! I have to find it now more than ever!" Zealously said and continued looking over and there for it.

"Listen Hunch . . ."

But Hunch was not stopping doing fast movements, looking around.

"Listen! In few minutes the show will begin and I want you in with us." Strictly told him.

"I have to find it! Do you not understand that it was right here!" showing him the spot.

"Yes I do. But it may be felt somewhere" Hunch cut him off.

"It did not!"

"Ok. It did not. Maybe then, someone else from us took it when you were not looking." Trying to give another reasonable explanation to calm him down.

"Nobody else was here and Jim has any right to put the blame on me." His voice sounded sad.

"I believe you ok? You say you did not take it then you didn't. Will you come inside?" pleaded him and he went back in.

Hunch did not respond on Ioanni's last words.

He continued.

"Jim! You should stop saying that he took it, He lost it now and he is acting like mad, plowing the yard up and down.

"Do not take his side now! He took it!" Jim answered. Behind them in the kitchen, in an old hand made chair, Nick was eating. He was having his dinner which it was milk with serials. His eyes met Ioanni's and a huge smile draw on his face.

"You did it! You hide our mobiles!" Ioannis pointed him.

"B-but . . ." Nick stammered and milk drop of his mouth.

"There is no but . . ."

"It is impossible for him to have done it. He was here eating this whole time." Jim supported him.

Nick was having the smile till his ears and he stood up from the chair doing a quick dance, shitting back down again.

Jim exchanged looks with Ioanni. His eyes talked to him and ensured him for Nick's innocence. He was doing pranks and he was the kind of guy who would tease with bad jokes. However not this time. Nick was his normal self and he was not hiding behind curtains. Acting alike and smiling meant only that he was happy, not he had something to do with the phones.

Although they needed answers, Nick could not help them. Accusations were still on Hunch's back.

"It is the shepherd!" Void with a humorous and not voice said.

"He he. Why not." Jim continued with the joke.

Just entering the house, Hunch heard the name "shepherd" and with no restrains began laughing, thinking that they were not holding a grudge against him anymore.

He was mistaking.

Jim turned his eyes on him violently. Hunch felt a haunting aura around Jim enclosing him.

"Why are you laughing, will you please explain me?" Ioannis asked him gently.

"Why, indeed?" Jim enquired him more strictly.

Hunch paused.

"You said you have nothing to do with it. What if someone else came and took them whilst we were not looking?"

Hunch remained silent.

"You do not laugh anymore hu?" Jim gave him another wild look.

"Let him be. Maybe they are all together in this, making a joke on the two of us. You know how they are. Forget about it and let's enjoy the night. I am sure we will have them before the end of the day." His words deeply serious.

"It is not so much about the mobiles but about him! I do not want HE to believe that he can trick ME!" Jim was afraid only for Hunch making fun of him in case he was behind it. In the past, Jim had done some pretty smart testes on him, proving to everyone that Hunch was not clever at all. Under no account he wanted Hunch to seem smarter than him at any case.

Jim had this issue, which he used to believe he was always right, with knowledge about everything. He didn't like to lose, as he was trying all the time to put his best in everything he was doing and certainly he didn't like from people he believed they were lower than him in capacity or elegance, to try to be superior. He had several fights for this reason in his life but he would never stop doing it. He was the oldest in the group but his actions were not making him look like his age.

"Mina san. Greece got talent is starting in a few minutes! Please come in the central bedroom to watch it." Ioannis with a loud voice called everyone to join him using a Japanese word for "everyone".

The two of them, Void and Hunch, were trying to figure out why the phone was not working. Times to times, Void was going under control, making panicked movements.

On the living room, Mr. Snake had not stopped playing with the x-box. Ioannis went near him and told him.

"Will you shut it down and come in? In few minutes it will start."

"Yes bro. I will come when I finish this game" quickly answered him, mind consecrated on the screen.

"Ioanni! Listen! I have a good one!" Jim yelled.

Ioannis extended his back and watched him from the living room.

Waiting for Jim to tell him.

"Hunch said he needs a screwdriver to fix the phone!" and Hunch's laugh filled the house. Even though he was studding it, it could be amazing to fix the phone since he was not good at it at all.

Tony wore his pajamas, ready to watch the show. He had missed not even a single episode and this season was the best. The mystery for the winner was great.

They were preparing the house for the night as well. Locking the windows and putting covers on the beds.

***** ***** ***** ***** ***** ***** ***** ***** *****

The small bedroom with the television had been prepared for the seven friends to watch the show. The pillows in the sofa were ordered in a way so everyone to find it comfortable to sit and the bed was no different than the sofa. Ioannis wanted everything to be perfect and he had made the room ready for a pleasuring night.

The sun was all the more hiding behind the graphic mountains. Although it was twenty to nine, the sun's light was their main source of light. There was no need still to turn on lights as summer makes day longer.

"Who wants pizza?" Void asked.

"I want some." Hunch said and Ioannis started touching his hunch.

"The phone doesn't work and its pure coincidence that you Hunch are studying telecommunications, hu?" Jim gave him a suspicious look.

Hunch smiled this time. They had no evidence he had something to do with the phones so he stopped worrying about Jim. Ioannis told him he believed him and this was enough.

"It is a great pizza!" Void popped up.

"And as I was already saying. He is the only one with knowledge over phones and the phones are gone. There is nothing else for me to say" held and gone.

"I am the ghost of the shepherd!!!" Ioannis changed his voice to sound spookier.

Smiles exchanged between everyone, including Hunch.

"I need some water. Can I drink form here?" Hunch enquired.

"This pizza is amazing." Void kept repeating.

No one seemed to have worries about the missing mobiles or the dead landline phone. Everything was going well for them, normal.

"Keep some slices for me too!" Mr. Snake who was playing pro-evolution soccer on the x-box, shouted from the living room. Nick with Mr. Snake refusing to watch the show, preferring to stay in the living room and play x-box, apologized to Ioanni for not watching it with them and stayed alone at the living room. The others of course, having pizza and coca cola, were ready for watching the Final of Greece Got Talent. Naturally Ioannis hated those two who decided to do not participate but he could not make them do it if they didn't want to.

In the double size bed Hunch was lying. Next to the bed in the sofa were Jim, Void and Tony. Ioannis sat on the edge of the bed without blocking Hunch's vision. The show was about to begin and all were having an excessive time.

As the commercials were still going on, Jim mentioned it again.

"I know why you do not worry about the phones. Because you are behind it."

"I am not worried because I know that someone else other than me has done it. Maybe it is you after all and you only want to blame me because you do not like me that much." Hunch defended himself.

"Why then, if I took all the mobiles, left yours? And do not say that I did it so as to blame you for having it and us for not." Jim attacked him again.

Only that this time Hunch smiled.

"I do not have my mobile too!" said and stared at him.

"Why are you lying? You were having it all this time on your waist bag" he had it most of the time with him.

"I am not. You are welcome to have a look." Jim did search it and he could not find it.

"Wait, does that mean we have no mobiles at all? No phones?" Void clearly panicked again asked.

"It is you Hunch and I know that you are behind it! You think you are smarter than us?" Jim attacked him once more.

"I have nothing to do with all that! We do not have our mobiles and instead of focusing to the problem you are still accusing me!"

"Yes! Because you took mine and everyone else's and you want to be smarter than us. Thing which is not going to happen!" he said, anger building.

"I did not want to be smarter than any of you. For me, certainly, Void, Mr. Snake and Nick didn't take them. But Ioannis you and Tony, you three are suspicious!" Finally blurred out.

"I took them, I confess, you found me." Tony said motionless.

"Point is that we have nothing to contact other people. That's it." Hunch stated and Ioannis took over.

"Now that you idiots found out that all the mobiles are gone, can we watch the show in peace and resolve this later?" Firmly said.

They obeyed. After all, someone among them should have taken them.

Right?

Ioannis gave a last shot, screaming a couple of times, so Nick and Mr. Snake in case he could convince them to join them but with no effect. So it started and night fell upon the sky.

CHAPTER THREE

NIGHT

The show was already in the half, showing a person who was doing silent comedy. They were speaking loud and shouting with each other for no reason. Talking in this way was making the night manlier. As for Nick and Mr. Snake, Ioannis was holding a grudge against them for not joining them. They were playing an hour now with the console and they really could go on playing all night.

Apart from those two at least, all the rest were there, watching it pleasantly.

"I do not think that he is going to win." Jim said.

"No one cares of what you think." Ioannis with his usual bad attitude shut him down.

"I believe that he is going to win. He was really good and he deserves it." Hunch also added.

"I haven't watched all the episodes but I can say that this year it had the best, I believe, talents." Void said for the sake of the conversation.

"I cannot believe that we are finally here. It is a great night!" Hunch confessed happy. Although he had passed a lot during the day, from bad jokes to unfair accusations, he was happy he had friends around him and finally this was THE moment. Trusting Ioanni for the night was a wise decision. Despite the fact he had lost most of his spirit as a result of the breaking up, he could still create nice events for his friends.

Maybe no one could see it, but for him as well as Hunch, friends were important.

Hunch was smiling and holding his fist from joy, and then, a smashing noise heard from outside. It took him a second to wake up from his dreamy thoughts and when he did, automatically turned his head to the side of the window.

No one else seemed to care.

In the room they were, the window was in the same high as the floor of the back yard.

"Oh! Guys! Did you hear that?" Full of wonder asked.

Everyone was laughing extremely loud with the show and naturally because of the noise they were creating, had heard nothing.

"Did you hear that?" he asked once again. They still went on ignoring him.

"Guys! DID YOU HEAR THAT!" repeated his words again, louder this time.

"What?" Jim responded first.

"A noise came from the window." With his mouth opened and smiling from the surprise.

"Yes. It was the headless horseman." Jim laughed on him.

"What exactly did you hear?" Ioannis with a hateful tone asked him.

"Something like someone threw a stone on the window."

"It was the magician from the previous act of the show. He turned real and came to eat you!" Tony added funnily.

They began laughing again.

Ioannis did not take him seriously but at least, he had nothing to lose by checking. He stepped on the bed and he opened the window. What he saw outside, on the ledge of the window, triggered his curiosity. A small candle was illuminating right outside of the window.

"What is happening, what is happening!" Hunch amused queried.

"It is the headless horseman. I won't say it again." Jim continued joking around. Everyone was laughing with the show and with the fun they were making to Hunch.

But the jokes were about to end unpleasantly once Ioannis saw that out of nowhere candle.

"What is that?" he said with query and his face indicated surprise.

"What!" Hunch full of joy stood from the bed and went to have a look.

"What happened?" Jim wondered too and the smile on his lips started fainting away. Tony approached the bed as well and he saw the light of the candle.

"Where is this light coming from?" Tony asked first, seeing light coming from outside.

The back yard was between abandon houses and there was no other source of light around apart from the house.

"Oh Oh! This doesn't exist! Look! Look!" Hunch pointed with his finger the candle to Tony and he was talking like he had won the lottery. The sense of unknown had turned his emotions high jumping.

"Get off the bed! It can take more all that weight!" Ioannis screamed and both Tony and Hunch distant from it.

"This is a historical moment!" Hunch said gloriously with his annoying smiling tone voice. Jim and Void went have a look too.

"Is this for real? A candle appeared ready just like that?" Ioannis began questioning.

How that was even possible?

"He he. Come on. This is not happening!" Jim not being able to believe it doubted.

"Morons! Come into the bedroom! Something out of the ordinary happened!" Ioannis run and called Nick and Mr. Snake. They looked each other and gave a though before they pause the game. But in the end, they did it and went after Ioanni.

"What?" Mr. Snake with agony asked.

"We were watching the show and suddenly Hunch heard something. I do not know what. He is the only one who had heard it. Like someone threw a stone or something. And I opened the window and a ready candle was there!" Ioannis gasped.

"What?" Nick concerned said.

"Come and have a look if you do not believe us!" Ioannis in an attempt to make them believe said.

Everything was becoming weirder from this point now.

"If this is a joke I will fuck you!" Nick without believing it said irritated. He liked to make jokes but if the jokes were on him, he was a bad receiver.

"Come here, come here." Hunch still on the bed called Nick to see the candle. The excitement of the moment had turned Hunch into a child discovering toys. That much his ecstasy was.

"We didn't do anything! You think that we have time for pranks now?" Ioannis said and Jim gave him a side look.

"You see it!? It appeared out of nowhere!" Hunch utterly surprised showed to Nick.

"I do not believe it . . ." Nick whispered.

"My, my . . ." Mr. Snake had a look too.

And he added as well.

"Again it is not what I was expecting." Sharp talking.

"What! You are not surprised at all?" Hunch marvelously surprised asked him.

Mr. Snake shrugged.

"Maybe the grandpa or the grandma left it like this before the leave the house." Nick made a hypothesis.

The house it wasn't empty all the year. It normally belonged to Ioannis and Tony's Grandparents. But for the summer, they have allowed them to stay alone with their friends. They were having another residency, in the town were the auntie and Void lived, living there occasionally. As the boys pleased their grandparents to stay alone in the house, the elderly had not objection.

"Someone lighted it now. Do not be stupid!" Jim blamed them for talking before thinking. The light was full and this was a sign that someone had just lighted it.

Void and Tony suddenly screamed. It was a scream out of wonder. Someone has done something in the show and they found it very interesting.

"Are you kidding me? You are still watching the show?" Nick asked with query.

"Why? Are you better? All this time you are playing video games?" Jim could not stand without talk.

The scene was turning red but Hunch stopped them before they start fighting.

"Shhh. Do you hear that? The dogs are barking madly." Hunch ceased them and everyone tried to listen at the barking dogs. The barking was so loud and it sounded at all the village. That kind of barking was not normal. And the fact that it was night was making it weirder. Void and Tony, lowered the volume on the TV but without stopping watching the show. The others were eavesdropping carefully the sound of the barking.

It sounded nearer.

They could not move for the sound was too captive.

As it came closer it stopped.

"We were all the time here! No one moved. Am I wrong?" Jim asked Nick, asking indirectly for Hunch's consent.

"No! No one!" Hunch quickly responded.

"If this is a prank, really, you are all traitors!" Nick sounded for first time serious. The chrome on his voice was sign of premature fear. His cheeks flushed and his eyes twinkled.

"Shall I catch it or shall I leave the candle there?" Jim frightened pointed out.

"Are you for real?" Nick surprised said.

"What if it has bullshits on it? Leave it. Do not touch it." Tony out of blue answered while he was still watching the show. Next to him, Mr. Snake had joined him. Somehow, Tony Void and Mr. Snake were not surprised with the appearance of the candle. This or they really did not find it odd.

"Hunch! Follow me outside." Ioannis demanded. Jim and Hunch, both, wear their flip flops with purpose on going in the back yard.

"What do you believe that the candle can have?" Nick questioned Tony.

"I don't know. But you see a lighted candle without knowing who left it and you are touching it?" He was having a point for not touching the candle.

Tony was never acting impulsive. He was the son of his father. He was serious and before he does something, it could take deep thoughts to act so.

His it was the difference from him and his brother and the case of fighting all the time when they were younger. Ioannis had nothing in common with his parents on their characters, or better, he may had both of his parents characters fused together, making him again individual. Tony was looking at a problem from all the aspects but most of the times, he was choosing wrong. Ioannis did not need time to think. He was more the acting person. That is the reason why during their childhood, they had fights because they were in trouble. Tony's wrong valuation of the situation and Ioannis's impulsive acting, were always putting them before their parent's judgment.

Now things were different. They had grown up and the fights were over. Tony was becoming more and more capable of judging right and valuates a problem from the right aspect and Ioannis was not as impulsive as it used to be.

A fair question came from one's mouth.

"But . . . We can go out from the window. Why to do the round?" Hunch queried stepping out of the room, coming closer to the entrance door. He made a small laugh, finding unreasonable what they were about to do. The window of the room was at the same exactly high as the back yard. If simple had opened the window they could pass to the back yard and not only, was the candle in front of their eyes but they could also touch it form inside the house.

"Because." Ioannis did not have to say another word for Hunch to stop laughing and tail him.

"Jim, take the flashlight please." Ioannis commanded him. Jim took from one table that was on the hall the flash light and before he goes out he returned at the room and raised a denunciation.

"I hope that neither you Nick nor you Mr. Snake did it!"

"Are you joking?" Nick insulted said.

His face turned irate.

"They could not have done it. They didn't want to leave the video game not even for a second. You saw them. Surefire they have nothing to do with that." Jim guaranteed for their innocence.

Ioannis had nothing else to add. He nodded Jim to finally follow him outside with the flashlight.

The beam was not powerful enough to light proper the way to the back yard but Ioannis had spent lots of years from his childhood in that house and he knew the path by heart. Apart from the insanely strong wind which was coming times to times, (villages on mountains have unexpected forces of winds coming and going any time) this night had, no other sound drilling nearby. As they were going closer to the window, the voices of their friends were the first thing to break the muteness.

And there was it, the candle, all alone and no one around there. The light from the flashlight was unnecessary now for the light of the house was plenty. They heard from the inside Hunch saying that they were living astonishment moments and Void answering him supporting words.

"Now I will show them!" Ioannis said malevolently and stroked a punch on the window. Everyone in the bedroom got scared and they began asking loudly what the noise was.

"Hahahaha . . . ." Jim started laughing silently. His eyes fixed on Ioanni, waiting for his next trick.

"Assholes!" Tony growled from the room, as he realized that it was no other than them.

They were not the only ones who got scared by the noise his fist made on the window. Hunch who was following, had been scared too.

"You deserved it!" Ioannis said satisfied.

The main reason they have been outside was not to have a better look on the candle but to look around for the guild. Someone had put the candle there and maybe that someone was still around there. They needed to be certain to avoid any repeating action like this.

They searched the back yard warily, trying to do not leave any place unspotted.

It seemed everything was clear. Whoever had done this now was gone.

"Seriously now, how did that happened?" Ioannis asked Jim.

"I do not know." He said while thinking. The though which was on his head was only one. Should they take this seriously from now on or to continue as a joke?

The others were watching the show. As the final, it was longer than the previous episodes, it need more time to finish.

Jim, Hunch and Ioannis returned back inside.

Ioannis sat on the sofa and gazed with an opened mouth. He was gazing at Hunch who was standing opposite to him smiling like an idiot. He was keep saying that he was overexcited and he liked it from the bottom of his heart. Mysterious happenings always intrigued his interest, he kept saying. For Ioanni was not a big deal this candle but he hated the fact that Hunch was acting so frenzied. They knew each other from middle school but they started their friendship at the end of high school.

Things for Hunch were always difficult. Even when he was a teenager, he had the hunch and he used to be a lot fatter. All the other kids despite him for that and they were not talking to him. He was lucky in one thing. He had never been abused by anyone. He may had no friends but at least they were not teasing him as well. Once the high school ended, Ioannis approached him. He was the first boy ever invited him on his house. Day after day, Hunch came close to Ioanni and they became friends.

Ioannis knew who he was and he was the kind of person he liked to help someone. He knew that Hunch, despite his appearance was a good person and for this, he wanted him on his party. The problem was that he didn't know his deeper problems. Hunch was light minded. His brain was working properly, not dysfunctional, but he was not and the smarter person in the world. As the years past, Hunch's stupidity sometimes caused problems and that is why they began treating him badly, considering him as an idiot.

This time was no different. Hunch being amazed by all this, was acting too suspicious. For something unexpected like a candle to appear, Hunch should be more frightened than laughing around. Thing which was making Ioanni outrageous.

You are the only one who laughs you know that?" said venturous.

Hunch offered him another smile only this time it appeared scared. Candles may not frighten him but Ioannis certainly was.

In the living room, Nick with Mr. Snake continuing the match they have left in the middle. Those two were able, even if the world was destroying to finish first their game and then to run for their lives.

As the show was going on, Tony and Void were the only ones who were actually watching it. Ioannis was already too skeptical and Hunch was still too excited to stay still watching TV.

Something triggered Ioannis attention. He quickly stood from the sofa and started looking in every room of the house. Void observed that he was unease and he asked him what was going on with an unmistakable trace of agony.

"Jim . . . Jim is not in the house." His voice was a dry leaf crackle. Not able to believe that he wasn't around, went and ask Nick if they have seen it.

"I think that he is in the toilet." Nick said tensing as he was playing, not taking his eyes from the screen.

"He is a grand shit machine. Where else he could be." Mr. Snake generously added without taking his eyes from the screen as well.

"It's about time we got serious." Ioannis blurted out.

Nick turned his head on him and looked at him as he was hypnotism. His eyes, after playing for that long had turned red and his brain apparently had started going numb.

"Stop playing and concentrate on what is happening around you!" he pressed them.

"Relax man. Everything will be fine. The match soon will be over." Mr. Snake tried to comfort him.

"Jim! Jim!" Ioannis started yelling while he was going to the toilet to find him.

However, he was getting no response.

"HEY BALD ASSHOLE!" As a last result shouted. He didn't make it till the bathroom and Hunch was behind him with his annoying smile.

"He is doing it for fun. I am sure that he wants us to be scared." He hissed and his mouth was on its favorite shape. Corners turned up.

This smile was something more than annoying, it was disgusting. Ioannis suggested him impatiently to stop smiling otherwise he would punch him right on his teeth.

Once more, Hunch leaned his head, looking on the floor. He was mildly discomforted by this way of menace.

"Jimmy boy!" Tony cupped his hands around his mouth and screamed.

"Where is he after all?" Mr. Snake asked. He and Nick had finally finished playing the eternal match. It was dark everywhere because the lights of the house have been switched off. They preferred watching television in pitch black.

"Switch on the lights now! This joke has to end now!" Ioannis commanded.

"Shall I switch this one?" Tony inquired, pointing the one on the kitchen.

"What about the show?" Void without really carrying about the show asked Ioanni.

"Forget about the show. We can still watch it on YouTube." The lights switched on by Tony and the scene became clearer.

The guitar, the sofa, Nick's and Hunch's luggage, everything seemed normal. But Jim was certainly not in the room.

Hunch chuckled and Ioannis riotously looked at him waiting for his silence. Hunch sensed that his stupid laughs were making Ioanni crazy and he instantly turned grim, gazing at the floor again, like a dog that had just being punished.

"All the mobiles are gone! Whoever took them shall talk now!" Ioannis said genuinely pissed. What he was feeling was a weird sensation. Half of him was afraid, and the other half surged with anger. Nick and Mr. Snake were sitting on two big armchairs before the television with the game console on the living room. Ioannis exasperated yelling on them, accusing of them missing mobiles. He knew that they haven't taken them but he couldn't stay still any longer and act like there was nothing to worry about. They all gathered at the living room for being too awkward, hearing Ioanni so outrageous.

"Please! If any of you have taken my mobile it would be good to give it back! My mother definitely will be looking for me!" Void repeated his previous worries, sounded troubled touching his head with both of his hands.

"Just a second. My mobile is definitely inside where we were watching the show. It should be still there." Tony pointed at the bedroom and he did it so as Hunch see him.

"That is true! Let's go and take it!" Hunch splendidly said. The two of them left, heading at the room.

"Can we?" Mr. Snake was about to say to play more with Nick, showing him the console. But as expected, Ioannis told them to do not talk, in an impolite way.

"Hahahaha!" Hunch laughs were bouncing on the walls of the house, and Ioannis angrily run on him.

"Why you galactic idiot laughing again?" he said to Hunch and his voice spilled blood.

"I did not find my mobile but on its place, I found two euros!" Tony said amazed and he raised his hands with the two euros coin showing it at him. Ioannis was at this moment flabbergasted. Apparently they all had a good mood but they were forgetting that a candle had appeared out of nowhere and that Jim was not in the house.

"Morons, stop the prank now! Where is Jim?" Nick all of a sudden worried rose as a question.

"Why you ask? He is not in the toilet?" Mr. Snake followed right behind him.

"No!"

"Jim! Jim! WHERE ARE YOU?" Ioannis started shouting his name. He even got outside on the yard screaming his name. Unsurprisingly, he got no respond. He went fast back in and made a suggestion.

"Who wants to come outside and look for him?"

"Come on boss. He is doing it for fun. To scare us." Hunch believed that Jim was doing this as revenge. Jim believed that Hunch was the one who had taken the mobiles and for that, he wanted to see Hunch frightened as an equal revenge.

This was at least what was on Hunch's head.

"If it is as you say, let us all go out search for him and if we find him, we will punish him for his doings. Do you agree?" Ioannis told him knowing that, whatever he would tell him, he wouldn't make him change his mind on believing that he was doing it to scare them. Stubborn people are hard to compete with, especially in Hunch's case which he was also second minded.

"Dress up and follow me outside quickly!" Ioannis coaxed

"I will take a jacket with me as well. It may be summer but at night is always colder than the day." Tony said hoarsely, having something on his throat.

"Wait for us to be ready too." Nick reminded them while he was putting his shoes on. Hunch was doing the same thing both sitting on the TV-bedroom.

"How come and you are the only one you heard the noise?" Nick asked Hunch politely.

"I do not know. Maybe because I was closer to the window than the others? I don't know"

"Hm . . ." Nick forced a smile.

"What?" Hunch smiled back.

"Will you tell me how the candle appeared there?"

"I don't know. But I will tell you this. I am the only one who heard the noise in the window not only because I was close to it but I also think that the others were too concentrated watching the show." He told him and he nodded. Ioannis walked that time into the room and heard the small chat.

"I have a bad feeling . . ." he added and exhaled.

"It is the second advent of Christ!" Hunch said and for a second in sounded like he really believed it. Although it was a non-sense theory, it was the first sign that he was taking it seriously. This entire time his was joking with the mobiles, with the phone, with everything, including that day. At least now, he had started fitting more in the situation. Something was odd this night and he had just started realizing it.

"If this is no magic, then I do not know. Power of God maybe?" Hunch persisted that this had something to do with God.

"I forgot to take off my glasses." Mr. Snake mumbled while passing near them.

He was wearing the glasses only when he was in front of a screen. Hunch sounded from the room, hissing Nick for not having his shoes yet. Nick was telling him that he was scared and he was not sure weather was a good idea to go outside or not.

"Nick is . . ." Mr. Snake tried to say something to Ioanni but he got silenced before he did.

"Do not speak that loud. We have to go out and let Nick do his things. Jim has to be found. I am not afraid and have faith. Everything is going to be alight."

"Ok." Mr. Snake agreed and backed off.

Ioannis turned his head to the TV-bedroom.

"I will not say it again. Do fast and stop messing around. We have to go!" patience was something that Ioannis never had, especially on times like this. For him, time was important. Some people have it since birth, to do not be able to lose a minute. Wasting time for no reason makes these people even more impatient causing them sudden anger.

This was one of these cases now. The more they were taking their time, the more Ioannis becoming angrier. He could not understand why they needed so much time for something as simple as wearing their shoes on.

"Where is the pizza?" Mr. Snake not having eaten a lot cause of the video game asked hungry. Hunch looked at Nick and laughed. He hid it from Ioanni because he knew he could be outrageous if he was seeing him laughing again. The opened mouth exposed Hunch's ugly from the dirtiness teeth. He had a good personality but all the somatic abnormalities sideways with his stupidity, were not helping him to go out of the center of mockery. An example at the time was his teeth. He did not have a disease but he had poor memory. He was not brushing them often and as a result, his teeth were most of the times dirty. And that it was not the only problem he had. Unfortunately for him, he had a huge mouth and when he was laughing or yawing, you could see flawlessly his muddiness.

Nick soured his face from the view and he met his eyes with Ioanni. Before he reacts, he directly told him.

"Listen Nick, should you be scared, stay here to guard the house!" Ioannis did not seem to have the time now to deal with Hunch's problems as they were running bigger ones.

"There is no way to do it. To stay here alone!" and his voice trembled.

"This village is deserted. Only few villagers are living here now. There is luckily for thieves to have come here!" Ioannis sounded alert.

"My mother will be looking for me!" Void's constant concern sounded from the living room.

"That is also another proof of something weird is going on. Where all the mobiles are?" Excitedly this time said.

"My mother will have already called me ten times by now! I am certain!" Void comprehended said and terror made the situation surreal. The fact they had nothing to communicate with, seemed like no joke as things were becoming anomalous.

"If you are all ready, search for flashlights around the house and let us leave!" Ioannis eyes darted to all of them, who they had just now gathered at the living room. They started looking around for flashlights or any kind of light devices.

"I will search inside the drawers of my bedroom. I haven't examined there yet." Tony willing added and went to search. He had no luck. There was none flashlight. He walked back and he entered the living room again. The air was tensed in the living room.

It was Mr. Snake now, who was having an apprehensively question-answer chat with Hunch.

"My mobile has gone long time now." Tony heard Hunch telling Mr. Snake.

"You do not have it too?" Mr. Snake questioned astounded Ioannis was walking up side down the room.

Hunch nodded.

"I am the one that lost it first." Ioannis told them while eating his nails.

"I have a feeling that your mobile cousin, is in my house. But even if you have forgotten it there, doesn't explain where the rest of the mobiles are." Void stated, being right.

The atmosphere was shifting minute by minute. Fear was enclosing them. All the mobiles have gone and they had nothing to communicate. Let alone Jim was absent not knowing eventually if he was trying to scare them or if something had really happened to him. The beat in their hearts, was gradually becoming faster. Nick was suggesting, not only taking flashlights but knifes too. Although he made the suggestion, he could not be heard because Hunch was talking over his voice.

"There is no way Jim doing such a prank!" utterly and without mistaken declared.

For one more time, someone cut Hunch off from talking and took the speech. It was none other than Ioanni.

"We have only one flashlight. Tony, take Hunch . . ." he started trembling and losing his words. He tried to say something, but it slipped his lips and made no sense. Rapidly, he corrected it, talking normal again.

"He will first search around here. There behind the cliff, there is an old small cabin which I want to go and check. If he is hiding in that place I will find him easily cause there is nowhere to really hide in there. Though I doubt he will be there . . ."

"And we can search in the back yard and in the old houses! There is high chance him, hiding in there too. Before he disappears wasn't he there with you?" Void added.

"Yes he was behind us and then we lost him when we came inside." Hunch replied confirmative.

***** ***** ***** ***** ***** ***** ***** ***** *****

As entering in the front yard from the gate, the house was at first sight. On your left hand, standing looking at the house was the road. An old stoned one but still very tough. One side of this road was leading to the high way through a mountain and the other side was leading to the village.

On your right hand were two visible areas. The first one was an old abandon cabin. The grandparents used to store woods for the fire in there as well as keeping the donkeys. This of course was years before this generation. The last ten years was only a storage house. It had all the equipment for gardening and the parents of the brothers had also made a separate room for old furniture they were not using anymore.

Next to it now, there was another smaller gate. This gate was leading to the mountain and to the back yard.

The have stopped using the path to the mountain from this gate because it was too anomalous. But the way to the back yard was in perfect condition. Walking to the back yard there were two things you could see. One on your left was another house's back yard. This house was not in use for years so the parents, didn't not take any caution building a fence between the two houses. In front of the back yard, a toilet was and a room where the generator for the heating was stored.

Going to the right now where more things to see. Two houses, two abandoned and rotten houses with an old stoned oven and a small yard. These two houses used to be the houses where the grandfather grew up. They were his main resident. With the years, he build another house, the one they were in now, and those two since no one was using them, got old and rotten with the time. Now they were not even inhabitable.

Last place they owed was a small coop on the mountain side of the front yard. This coop was as old as the two houses and as dirty as a stable. Plants had grown up inside the walls and old dirty scraps from the animals living there were still on the floor. No one mind all these years to clean it. Time swallowed it as it had done pretty much with all the village.

***** ***** ***** ***** ***** ***** ***** ***** *****

"Take flashlights with you! It is dark outside now and we will need them." Tony said.

"Where is the flashlight we used before?" Ioannis asked looking for it.

"It is here, I found it!" Void said showing it to him.

"Perfect! Let's go and find him now." Hunch enthusiastic for the adventure to begin said.

"Why is he so happy?" Mr. Snake whispered at Ioannis ear.

"I do not know . . ." he replied making a face.

"Actually, give me the flashlight. I will keep it." Mr. Snake asked from Void.

"Ok."

"You know what we can do to find him easier? We can shout his name as we are searching for him!" Hunch told Ioanni and Void, who they were first to the door, going out look for Jim.

They separated into teams of two. Ioannis changed his mind on going alone to the cabin. He team up with his cousin and they decided first a look in the old coop and then in the cabin. Hunch and Tony went together, taking the other root, to the back yard and the old houses. Ioannis said to Void to continue alone because he wanted to return to the house for some reason and he would be finding him inside the cabin in few minutes.

Nick and Mr. Snake stayed in the house, ensuring everything is fine and wait for Jim in case he decided to appear. Ioannis had just opened the door, entering in, and probed by Nick.

"Staying here is pointless Ioanni. It is better if we are out looking for him too."

"It will be faster if we do it all together. Let alone that I have the flashlight, I was ready to go out" Mr. Snake completed.

"So . . . Where shall I go to search?" Nick asked again.

"Could anything else possible go wrong today?" Ioannis muttered bad-temperedly to himself.

"Will you answer me?"

"Let's . . . . Let's go to Hunch and Tony." He muttered. Nick and Mr. Snake agreed, following him fast at the back yard. Unexpectedly, they heard them talking about something important.

"The candle . . . Is not shining anymore!" Hunch with a low, near to the ground voice said. Tony realized that his brother was there and took the chance to ask him if he had done this to the candle.

"Do not mind about stupid things like this. Most probably the wind extinguished it." Ioannis sneered and then went on.

"Void went alone to check at the coop." but Nick cut him off.

"I believe that we should better lock the house." He said and winced.

Mr. Snake lighted the extinguished candle with the flashlight's beam.

"What I am afraid the most are thieves. This village is hidden between mountains and as you already know, not so alive." Ioannis claimed.

"Where is the candle? I do not see it." Nick cut Ioanni off for a second time.

"I am lighting it . . . It right over there." Mr. Snake remarked.

"The candle is not shining anymore. And we asked who extinguished it and they said that no one of us did it." Hunch talking in trepidation, trying to explain Nick that the extinction of the candle was a very important element.

"Are they short of stupid? We just told them that it was the wind, didn't we?" Mr. Snake thought and gazed flicked across their faces.

When fear takes place, even the most unimportant and small things can turn into massive harms. The candle had probably gone off because of the wind. It was a candle after all in an open ground. But the way the night was evolving, fear or exhilaration of the supernatural, was mudding their judge.

"Please . . . can we go inside the house again?" Nick with a guttural voice asked.

"For me this candle should not be here in a first place. I do not believe that Jim is behind this and I certainly find it mysterious that the candle is off now." Hunch had given to the extinction of the candle too much importance.

"Alright, we will go back to the house and we will see how to deal with tonight." Ioannis decided.

Nick looked better now they were about to go back.

"Void, yo, Void!" Ioannis shouted. He was already heading to the front yard, having as a tail all the others following him behind.

"Cousin! Where are you?"

"Void! Void!" Nick and Mr. Snake followed Ioanni in the shouting.

"He most probably is inside the house." Mr. Snake made a notice.

"Just to warn you, we should better keep it low. Our voices I mean. I do not want to make noises now. It is safer to keep a low profile." Tony lightly scared pleaded.

"But . . . This is the opposite of what we were supposed to do. Should not we be shouting their names? For example for Jim, to shout, JIM JIM? You know." Hunch all query asked.

"We were shouting and nothing happened. Or you did not notice it idiot?" Ioannis as entering the house shouted, but with a low tone, at him.

On the table of the kitchen, Nick was grabbed a small bag with chips to eat as a snack. Mr. Snake saw him and his saliva drop of his mouth.

"Where is Void? Isn't he here?" Tony ventured to ask.

"Where is the pizza?" Mr. Snake did a question following Tony's question.

"He is not back yet?" Ioannis astonished asked and he stood his mouth opened for a second.

"No." Tony after looked in the house coolly answered.

Void was not in the house and he did not replied in the earlier calling too. This was not like him. Even if he was the youngest among them, he was more mature than anyone. For his age, he had the brain to think as an adult and to act with consideration. He knew the village as well as the brothers did, but it was impossible for him to do a prank. He was not into pranks, not to mention the fact he was scared of the darkness. His absence was a sign that something had gone wrong when he was out looking for Jim, and this would not take long for the team to realize it, especially Hunch.

***** ***** ***** ***** ***** ***** ***** ***** *****

Things were getting weirder and weirder and a new situation came up. Nick hadn't noticed at first but he slowly realized that his and Hunch's luggage were both opened on the sofa. Hunch saw that and he widely opened his eyes, looking amazed and speechless. He stared at them spaced, now fixed on Nick and back in the luggage again. Unblinking and t the corners of his eyes the murk had started taking over the room. Patterns danced in his head, the table, the chairs, the window.

Blinking his eyes, he woke up from his stun.

"What is happening? Did anyone put his hands on your luggage?" Ioannis having notice it, worried asked and made a movement with his hand, to saw him that he was really concerned.

"It is open and a little bit messed up." Hunch's voice had an unease tone. Fast he closed them all in front of Nick who was standing astounded. Nick's luggage was not on the sofa were it should be, but on the contrary was on the floor. He had a really quick look before he closed them just to ensure everything were inside.

Nothing has been taken.

Tony from the kitchen advised Ioanni for locking the windows there or not.

"Bro! I will lock the windows here, is it ok?"

"There is no need to ask me for this! Just do it."
Apprehensively answered.

"I am taking all of my precious belongings with me!
Wallet keys . . . I don't like this hell situation!" Hunch
was cursing from the TV-bedroom and none could blame
him. He was afraid and pissed off, both emotions fusion
together. He put them all on a small blue waist bag he was
always carrying along.

"Let's, let's go till the kinder garden." Ioannis said fast,
his voice trembled.

They were gathering in the entrance hall without
realizing it. Tony was trying to lock correctly the window
on the kitchen but he was experiencing some difficulties.
Nick walked in and opened the refrigerator's door.

"You will take your things to move them where,
Hunch?" Nick standing before the refrigerator with a box
of juice on his hand asked him aggressively.

"I am sure that my cousin had headed this direction."
Ioannis chided. It was a familiar act, when someone else
was talking, to interrupt and speak no matter what.

"Money, credit cards . . . All those short of things. I
want to have them with me instead of leaving them here
unprotected." Hunch replied to Nick, who was not really
paying attention on him at the moment, drinking juice.

"We are going to the kinder garden, do you hear me?"
He raised his voiced as he was waiting on the door. Mr.
Snake went from the living room to the kitchen. Ioannis
saw him passing in front of his sight, blocking his view
on the other two.

"My luggage was opened! Do you believe it?" Nick
revealed impatiently.

"Seriously?" Mr. Snake with a pathetic voice replied
at him. They started talking and instead of going to the
door where Ioannis was, they went in the living room with
Tony. Ioannis exhaled and he went at the bedroom with
the television and the two tweaked luggage. He switched

off the TV which it was playing without anyone watching any longer, and he followed as well, irritated, on the living room. He was excepting them to go with all the patience he could at the moment. He was not sure himself either how he had borne it that long. Whether they were coming now or not, he had reached his limit.

"Do I have to say for a third time to follow me until the kinder garden? This becomes ridiculous." Obviously annoyed, that no one was listening on his commands, said.

His voice never reached them because Nick was yelling.

"This is not the only case we should worry about! Count and you will see!" Nick really seemed terrified and a patch of skin at his neck blushed.

"The mobiles . . . the missing mobiles and the missing people . . . two by now and who knows . . ." He continuing saying frightened, counting with his fingers showing how much scared he was, but Ioannis stopped him.

"You are right. But first of all, we have to go to the kinder garden to crisscross if they are there, trying to make fun on us. Do not forget that my cousin knows this village as well as I do. If somehow Jim had persuaded him to help him in a prank, they would have gone there because it is a safe place and they can do something to pass their time while we would be here, worrying for them like crazy." And he showed with his head at the door's way. He had to pass in a narrow space between the double bed and the table of the living room in order to go back to where he came from. He did it and the rest trailed.

"I am . . . ." Nick was about to add, but something in his voice did not let him. It had a tenor as he was ready to start crying. Before he does, Ioannis stopped, one step from the entrance hall.

"One last thing. If we see anyone . . . and I mean anyone. Do not talk to him about this until I say. In case they just want to scare us, it should be no good to serve ridicule. Is it ok Hunch?" concerned, asked the only person he was afraid the most. He looked on his eyes and Hunch agreed with his words nodding.

"Ah! We need the flashlights! Do not forget them!" Hunch said and sounded like a rescue ranger.

"Why the plural? We only have one." Ioannis mentioned. The sound of it frustrated Hunch. One flashlight, was barely enough for so many persons. If they wanted to be able to see in the kinder garden, they would need two at least. Where they were going, Hunch had spotted when he had gone with Nick earlier this afternoon, that there were no lights. Despite the fact he knew that, having two flashlights would be much better than one.

Without having the required courage to talk, he passed it.

Last thing they had to do was to make sure all the windows were locked and all the lights had been switched off. The windows on this house, especially the ones looking in the backyard, were easily violated since they were at the high of the ground. They should be absolutely certain, that by the time they come back, no one would have broken in. Turning off the lights, was essential too.

"Before you switch off the lights, mind to turn on the flashlight. We will not be able to see without light in here." Tony forestalled and said. They were all running inside the house like mad. To lock the windows, to turn off the lights, to find anything they could take with them. It was a pretty upsetting scene.

"Imagine, to return and our things to be missing." Nick said pale.

"Hey, hey! Why to turn off the lights is essential? If we are not home and there is no light, we make it easier for them. If we at least leave some lights on, they will consider twice coming in." Hunch had a point. He was afraid to accuse them for not taking a second flashlight but this time, what he had on mind he had to say it out loud.

"What to think twice? They did it with all the lights on and us inside. Do you think they will hesitate to do it if we leave just the lights on? Bullshits . . ." Nick objecting to Hunch said. At the same time they were talking, Tony said that he had found one more flash light and he was the one to keep it.

"First thing first. I will have one flash light, undisputable. Second thing now. I want the lights to be off. End of story. Is better and that is my decision." Ioannis said and put an end to this dialogue.

"After all, we have already turned them all off." Mr. Snake added in an attempt to say something significant.

"Where is your flashlight?" Tony asked his brother once he saw that he did not have anything.

"Is in . . . Are you an idiot? This is the one that I used before. You didn't find another?" he answered with his eyes closed because of the impotence he was seeing.

"No. I thought . . ."

"Whatever, I will not have one. You can have it. We will make it with only one. Can we FINALLY GO?" For one more time, Ioannis mentioned the fact he wanted them to leave the house and go search for the missing two. He was the first who opened the door to the yard. The rest were following him like a tail.

It was night time and the moon was taking secret peeps behind unrelated clouds which were coming and leaving. It was a goodbye to the day and a hello to the stars in heaven's great vast.

Tranquility and peace got interrupted by the five young men.

"If my cousin is missing too, then I am afraid that something terrible is really happening. He has to be in the kinder garden because it is the only place he could possible go, with or without Jim. In case he is not there I am already thinking the worse." He passed, went on.

"And we shall not forget about the shepherd as well . . . I do not believe it, of course. Maybe there are thieves or nothing at all. But if the legend is true even and in its tiniest part, we have to be aware!" Ioannis ended sending an extreme message to his friends.

"Wait a second!" Tony yelled while the others were out of the yard, down warding the street already.

"I will wait here!" Hunch stopped in the car that was parked outside of the house. He had a thought and he started to examine the car. He had a look on the left and a look on the right side of it. Everything seemed to be normal. Mr. Snake wanted to say something to Ioanni but Hunch interjected.

"Well . . . We will split into two groups . . ." and he was talking like a detective in a thriller movie. He even put his hand under his chin, starting rubbing it.

"Why to split up?" Ioannis asked incredulously. He wanted to make Hunch stop acting as a leader. Acting as he had all the answers, playing it smart, was more than annoying.

It was Hell!

Ioannis inwardly applauded.

"You are very smart. Now listen to me. We have to be as quite as we can. Try to do not make any noises." Ioannis said, letting him not finish his though.

"That is why you should lower your tone now, Hunch!" making it sound like he could not care less about his leading speech. Hunch did not say anything more. He followed his rule and stayed quiet.

Behind him a guttural voice asked.

"What is that over there!" and that was the voice of Nick.

He was looking at a church, far away, in the pick of a mountain. There was no way to discern the church from that distance, unless you knew already that one existed there.

"I saw a light!" said and start laughing. Could not hold it any longer.

They did not even try to reason Nick. They let him laughing without worrying.

"Tony, do not lock this door. Leave it unlocked. Just lock the house door and keep the keys." Ioannis was talking about the gate of the yard and Tony was just walking out of it at the moment. He did as he said and in chorus he noticed the motorbike, parked in a different place than before.

"Did you move it?" With a questioned face asked his brother.

Ioannis nodded.

"Jim is missing . . ." Hunch terrified said.

"And his cousin as well." Mr. Snake added, not letting him forget that.

"You do not want to put the motorbike in the yard?" Tony's eyes contracted his brother.

"No. It is heavy for us to lift it to put it inside. I don't believe anyway someone can steel it. Only with a track they can take it but if that is the case, we can hear a sound like that one and come back. We are not going that far. What the hell." His eyes flicked back to his brother.

They communicated using their eyes. They have grown up as good brothers.

Ioannis raised his finger in the air and pointed forward.

"Ikimashou!" he said in Japanese and he meant let's go.

***** ***** ***** ***** ***** ***** ***** ***** *****

Outside of the house, ready to go to find their friends, began walking the road to the kinder garden. They have only started and something suspicious made them stop and listen.

Wild barking all over the village.

Dogs were barking like possessed. As loud as they could. The echo in the mountains was absolute, making the barking even more horrifying. The sound of it was creating scary images on their heads.

"Oh!?" Hunch expressed.

"Even the dogs have started and . . ." Nick frowned and shook his head as a sign of testament that things were not normal.

"The thieves are one story. But what I am afraid the most is the stupid legend. I do not have any mood for a shepherd's ghost to appear and hunt us down." Ioannis tried to sound as passive as possible, though his heart was beating a double tempo in his heart.

"The thing is that your father is a very serious man and this story it has to be true at some point. I don't know . . ." Nick "ate" his words and didn't continue.

"I believe him. That is the problem my friend!" Ioannis said and his eyes martyred fear. He continued.

"Anyhow, if this is a prank, they have to be in the kindergarten because is the only place they know well in this village. This or the cemetery. But I strongly doubt if they went there. Is too scary especially at night time and my cousin doesn't have the guts to do it."

"True! They do not have anything else to go to. Even if they wanted, this will make no sense. They didn't run to hide but to scare us. That leaves us only one option. They are there, waiting for our arrival and surprise us with a scare tactic!" Nick undisputedly said.

"I will keep the flashlight. Ok?" Mr. Snake said.

"Sure. But now we don't need it. Save the batteries for later that we will have it in need. As you can see here, the pillars on the road are enough."

Among them, one had started sweating. Nick wanted to ask a question but he didn't want to hear the answer. In the end, he found the courage and did it.

"Did that shepherd, ever did anything to anyone?" and his tone took a sudden trembling turn.

The barking was endless, becoming all the more wildly and loudly. The sound was closer to them, but they could not see any dog around.

"We don't know . . ." Tony answered honestly.

He flicked his eyes to Ioanni and he said to Nick.

"Truth is that we only have this incident heard from our father. He told us that but he knew about the legend. Other people have seen it too but they don't talk about it. As if someone had ever get hurt . . . I suppose we will never know, or we will." That was a scary way to finish his phrase.

Nick got his answer, which the same question Hunch also had.

Making a reference to the barking, Nick mentioned that the dogs are having one of the best instincts and that this has to be no good, barking like crazy.

"But why they do like this?" Hunch asked but the sound he make was barely audible, a feeble stirring in his throat.

"I have started to believe that this is an omen." Ioannis turned and replied at him. As they were walking down the road, something, a shadow maybe, was on their way.

"Switch on the flash light Snake! I think this is a dog!" Mr. Snake did not react as fast as Ioannis would like him to, so he yelled at him with a rushing voice.

"Switch on the flashlight you FUCKED UP!" with his last words, the beam of the flashlight showed up, giving its light straight ahead. Luckily, there was nothing ahead. Minds tricks, this time, was nothing uncommon.

A barking so loud and mad, as a dog escaped from hell sounded. Hunch more than the others, got socked.

"Silence!!! You animals!" Ioannis angry screamed at the way of the barking. He could not see any dogs around but with the echo in the village, any way he would choose to yell, his voice could reach any direction.

It was not really effective. The barking didn't stop, but this was the least of their problems.

There was a great downhill and at the end of the road, a café, the only and one that the village had. It was not only a café but food and beverage were served as well. Some villagers were sitting outside, talking with each other, enjoying the summer breeze which the night was offering.

"Do not forget what I have told you earlier. If they ask anything, we will behave naturally. They do not need to know about Jim and Void but because in villages they are curious, they may ask short of irrelevant things." Ioannis remind them.

No objection about that. They all agreed.

"I do not want to cause any trouble in case this is only a prank. Let alone that if we do take it seriously now, and it is a prank, they will laugh on us." Ioannis said and he didn't even bother asking if they agreed this time. On his mind, they had to do as he said.

They passed in front of them. They nodded and the villagers nodded back. Fortunately they did not even ask why they were heading out. It was not late but in a small village like this, even if you are walking alone at noon, they will ask you why and where.

Hunch was walking alone ahead, separately from the others. The excitement he was feeling was enormous. The same sensation from before have not vanished yet. Half of him was afraid due to the disappearances and the other half, excited for the unknown. Of course, at this point, the others did not want to lose him from their eyes, so they called him to slow down his steps and wait for them to be all together. He slowed his step, and as he was the first one getting close the kinder garden.

There was something he had to say.

"Erm . . . If they were in there, should not we hear at least something? It has deadly silence." And his voice slightly stammered.

He got no answer on his question.

Maybe there was nothing to answer to, or maybe they did not hear him. However, one thing was certain. They were all standing in the steps leading the kindergarten.

Small stoned steps, no more than ten, downward. Even though it was night, the place had some high poles, where they were beaming light on some spots of the garden.

With that small light, they could at least see where to head to and to discern some of the things existing on it.

An old immense tree, on the center and three swings for children opposite of it. Nearby, if you knew the place, you could see the basketball court. If someone had not been there before, this court was not easily to spot in the night. It was slightly abandoned and it didn't look as much as a basketball court. Because the village did not have people going there often, they were not maintaining it and it looked like a wild square. Some plants, because it was an open one, had also ridden on the baskets. Of course, during the day, lots of things were visible, but at night, you needed a flashlight to see more than that.

"I am scared. I do not want to go down there." Nick not carrying about his pride any longer, said.

"Do not be afraid girl. We are all together here. Nothing can happen!" Ioannis let out a shaky breath and did the first step.

"But I cannot see!" Nick raised for a second his voice. He was not feeling proud he was scared, but he also did not want something bad to happen to him.

"It's five of us! We will be alright, let alone the two of us knows martial arts!" Tony dynamically said to give courage to the team. Their steps on the gravel were making a rattler sound, not one of those you can ignore.

"In courage-you find no fear
And in courage no-weakness does appear
In courage-steps toward
Danger taken
And in courage-strength
Within awaken
In courage-a hero
Takes shape
And in courage-the villain can't escape
In courage-there is a call
To duty
And in courage-out of ugliness
Comes beauty."

Ioannis remembered a poem he had once read about courage and he thought to say it out loud for boosting Tony's though. Courage at that time was something vital for every single one of them. This night after all, had been proved, as a night full of surprises that had yet to end. As they were exploring the area, the sound of their voices, talking all together, was making a cloud of unconnected noise. Close to the swings, was a bench.

"Have a seat over here." Ioannis suggested. The sound of their steps, until they get there, was similar to the sound the feet of the soldiers makes, walking all in a company tuned under the same step.

"Before we sit here, can you please brighten with the flash light this bench? I do not want to put my butt on a birds dropping." Tony disgusted said.

"Seriously . . . ?" his brother told him with a trace of irony.

"Yes, give me the flash light." Tony demanded and snatched it from Mr. Snake.

He lighted the spot he wanted to and gave it back.

"And we do not have any mobile to communicate with someone." Hunch said and scratched his head.

"You first of all, should sit down." Ioannis said and caught Hunch from his shoulders, pressing him toward the ground, until he sat on the bench.

Tony was sitting on the right; next to him was Hunch who was sitting next to Nick, who was sitting next to Mr. Snake. They all sitting there, like students, ready to hear Ioannis speech. He was about to start speaking but there has been an interruption. He frowned his eyebrows to see better as the night was making it hard to discern things from distance.

He was looking at the church

It was typical in Greek villages, the church to be close to the kinder garden. And of course, a church as traditional as this one comes along with the cemetery, right behind of it.

Ioannis stopped and with a panicked voice said.

"I think I see something down there!" where he was looking, was a sliding gate where someone could enter the back yard of the church.

"It looks like a person." He continued. His eyes pinched on this direction.

"I volunteer to go and check!" Mr. Snake said and with speed steps he started walking further and further from them. He was charged with excitement of discovering the unknown. It was thrilling for everyone, if eventually they were running on something supernatural.

Mr. Snake was not the type of person involving into problems. He enjoyed staying home, playing video games, going out only to grab something to eat or to meet with friends. He had quite the peaceful life and he preferred to keep it like that. He was trying to avoid troubles of any kind by staying alone most of the time. But by doing that, he had a loss of his activeness. He was too neutral some times and as a result, he was missing the fun of his age.

Even when he had to go at school, he hated the fact he had to do it more than any other teenager on the world. If there was a way to get food by staying at home, playing video games and relaxing, he would be the first in line to get it.

He volunteered to go and check, thing which it was not compatible with his passive personality.

Ioannis yelled, asking him to do not be reckless. His voice never reached on his ears. He had already gone too far. Hunch with Nick, were really concerned and afraid for some reason. None could say that this night was not a night which everything was possible, from discovering a ghost to risking their own lives. But risking their own lives was the part where Nick and Hunch were afraid of.

"I really believe I see something moving over there!" Ioannis kept saying. But no sooner he realized, Hunch's face was stunned, like he had seen a ghost.

"What is it?" he asked him with query.

"Maybe is the one who talked to us when we came here earlier to play basketball?" Nick said but his voice became a blur of meaningless sounds. Fear had obviously started taking its effects. Hunch apparently, had the same though passing through his mind.

"Yes, yes! The Dracula from earlier. He came and talked to us!" Hunch terrified said.

"He was crazy!" Nick breathed.

"Very suspicious! He said something like: Later this very evening, I will take out my sheep. I do not recall the precise words but whatever he had said, seemed suspicious." And Hunch was trying to bring back on his memory the scene.

"I do not remember as well . . . . damn . . ." Nick followed Hunch's awareness.

"Fuck your stupid LEGENDS!" Ioannis felt his body going rigid.

"But why to take his sheep out at night?" and Tony sounded as though quizzed. He was marveling the fact, the "Dracula" said that. Usually, the shepherds take the sheep for grazing at dawn and not at night.

"I have heard that in lots of villages, they go out with the sheep at night. That is why I did not give attention on his talking at the time." Hunch marked, his words stiff.

"We can still see Mr. Snake. That is good." Tony mentioned. And his figure was still discerning from the church.

"I am telling you! I saw something moving down there! That, whatever it was and a sheep at night, is something that we should not take for granted. It is vibrant!" and Ioannis started making sounds of apprehension in his throat. He sounded pretty upset for someone who was not sure whether it was a joke made by his own friend or not. Ioannis had all this time doubts or, he sounded at least like having ones, whether something was going on or not. His reaction was a bit overestimated.

"I do not think we should let him go all by himself." Nick said and from the tone of his voice, he was like taking responsibility for letting him go alone.

"Where . . . Where is he! We do not see him anymore!" Hunch said, his voice sounded as something bad had already happened.

"There is no reason to be scared! Don't cause us undue alarm. He also has the flashlight with him, so . . . ." Ioannis answered on Hunch's fear. He had a look around and then he made one more suggestion similar to the one he had done before with Mr. Snake.

"Tony, go . . . . go back to the house. Maybe they have already returned and there is no need for us to worry anymore." Ioannis urged his brother to go, while at the same time Hunch was saying to Nick that he could not believe the dogs which were still barking as they were possessed. Tony in all this talking, stood up, he stretched his shoulders and said.

"Ok. I am going back to the house to see if they have returned. Is highly possible, this prank had already ended and we do not know it." Saying that, Hunch moved his hand showing his objection and he also completed with words.

"There is absolute no way, us, to let you go all alone! Someone has to come along."

"Listen. If you remember, there are people on the central square. I will be fine. It is not that far from here and there are lights on the streets all the way until home." Tony sustained his idea.

"No way!" Hunch insisted.

"But Tony is right." Nick joined in the argument.

"Oh Hunch! Come on. I will go running and I will be back in no time. Do not be ridiculous now." Tony's displeasure was obvious. He could not accept that his friend didn't have faith on him. Especially when he knew, he was his model.

"You are going back to the house and we will go to find Mr. Snake." Ioannis verbalized.

"Will I find you here again?" Tony asked.

"What?" Ioannis asked him back, not having heard his question because of the fuss Hunch was creating with his constant objections.

"We will meet here again right?"

"Why you do not go with him Nick?" Hunch afraid of losing one more friend pleaded.

"Are you for real Hunch!? You really believe that something bad can happen to my brother!?" Ioannis started getting mad with his constant denial.

"But . . ." Hunch felt a roll of despair and did to say something but Ioannis cut him off before he even starts his phrase.

"Jim maybe is missing but Tony is nothing like him." told him irritably.

His voice note serious than ever.

"I cannot believe that you are letting him go alone!" it was abnormal under two disappearances, Hunch to accept that they were willing to let Tony go back at the house alone.

"Do I have to tell you that THEY MAYBE JUST WANT TO SCARE US!? We are not sure if something is happening for real or not. Chill down you stupid brainless koala." Those Ioannis last words, made Hunch realize that he maybe had dramatized the whole thing too much. He filled his lungs with air and agreed with Ioannis plan shrugging gently.

He had just relaxed and a though like a thunder crossed his mind.

A though which put him back on the table of fear.

"But where is Mr. Snake!?" he sounded hysterical this time. Tony had just left and Ioannis had started moving with Nick to the direction of the church where the cemetery was too. Albeit Hunch raised the question, no one seemed to be interested on answering him. Not wanting to cause any more controversy than he already had, he followed.

"I believe that we have done wrong movements until now." Nick turned and said to Ioannis while they were walking on the gravel.

"So you agree with me?" Hunch asked flatly.

"I simple believe that we should be more careful."

"Exactly!" Hunch exited for finally having an ally said.

"Jim and Void, gone missing before we go out of the house. Do you believe that this was a "wrong movement" as well? Because we had nothing to do with that." Ioannis wanted to know.

"I do not know. I am just saying that we have split too much." Nick told Ioanni and from the way he said it, sounded as he was feeling panicked.

"Ok, ok. Let us take things from the start. First, we lose connection with any possible outside communication. No mobiles, no landline. Then a candle appears, and then someone had messed up with your bags." Ioannis said and he was trying to remember if he was missing something else. He loved to make references on the past events because he liked to put things on a line, making his life easier.

"The bag man, the bag! It was on the floor, messed up; ok only a bit, but still someone had disordered it. And it was closed! Not even opened!" Nick felt a tremor growing in his belly.

"Are you sure that it was closed? Because I cannot really recall if it was closed or not." Hunch told him and qualm colored his voice.

"I am a hundred percent certain! I am a hundred percent certain!" Nick repeated twice.

"No way! You killed me with that now!!!" Hunch suddenly got very surprised that the bag may be closed. He caught Nick from the arms and held him tightly. He took one second to think and then he said again calmly.

"But I am not really sure. I think that . . ."

"I am completely sure! I just left for some second and when I have returned, everything was disordered! I know I have closed it, because I had opened it to take a sweater before all this start!" and by saying that, Hunch cupped his hands on his mouth and covered it on the idea of something like this had really happened.

"I am socked now . . . Where is Mr. Snake? Why don't we scream his name?" he said.

"Why do you want me to yell? I am scared, fucked it!" Ioannis nervous told Hunch.

"We must not lose him too . . . what is happening now?" Hunch said and his voice was barely sounded. He did not know how to go against Ioannis when he was in this state.

"If something happened to him, I do not want to happen to me too!" Ioannis told him, his note calmer this time.

"You are right but we have to try and call him. That's what people do in situation like this."

"For fuck shake . . . OK then." Ioannis took a deep breath.

"Mr. Snake!!! Mr. Snake!!!!" and started screaming his name whiles all three walking closer to the church.

"Mr. Snake!!! Mr. Snake!!!" Hunch followed Ioannis example. Screaming his name, they drove out of the kinder garden and the sliding gate of the church, was within walking distance now.

The kinder garden had two entrances. One was the one they had come into and the other was right opposite of the church. It was not a door or anything. It was just a passage to get out. Five feet from there, was the church.

"There is light coming from the inside of the church . . . What the hell is going on?" Ioannis unbalanced placed.

"What are those three buildings?" Nick asked him when he saw three long cubed structures in the churches ground. They were one after the other, ending to the graveyard.

"I am not sure but I am not going further in." Ioannis answered and stopped before going into the yard.

Just in the sliding door which it was ajar.

"You are right. But shall we stay here?" Nick asked Ioanni, not having the will to act on his own.

"I am not going in there! I am telling you I saw someone standing right here, where we are now! I do not want to go any further!"

"Ok . . . but what about Mr. Snake?" Nick made Ioanni to close his eyes and think hard.

"Fuck you are right!!! If Mr. Snake gone missing here, then that means that we should also go inside! Damn!" Ioannis cursed through gritted teeth.

"No! I am not going anywhere near the church's ground!" Hunch said scared. The sky was stained dark and fragments of fear were covering the area.

"But if we do not go, how are we supposed to find him!?" Ioannis asked Hunch with lot of rage on his voice. Fear makes people become more violent than they use to be. Sometimes, it makes them reveal their true selves as well. Hunch not having the power to resist against Ioanni, passed the sliding gate and founded in the church's yard. Ioannis and Nick had already done the first move to proceed inside and he only had to follow them.

"If something has happened to him, I want to help him!" Nick said walking in circles.

"I prefer something bad to happen to me than to lose my friends!" Fear had taken its effect on Nick but compared to Ioanni who was roofed with anger, on Nick's case, was giving him courage. His true self, was beyond better than the one he was displaying under normal circumstances.

"Mr. Snake!" Ioannis screamed again while walking toward the cemetery. He passed all three constructions and he was seeing another gate but this one was different. This gate had a cross on its center. It was a gate which was opening by splitting into two pieces, a small double-gate. One piece was splitting on the left and one on the right, making the cross on the center half and half. Opposite the gate, it was a big and well preserved, grave of a priest.

"This is the cemetery . . ." Ioannis said as he showed the splitting gate.

"What are you talking about?" Nick with tremendous voice said but his question was not one that needed an answer. He knew that they were going to the graveyard but he had to say it in order to let some of his fear slip out.

"Mr . . . ." Ioannis was about to scream once again his name but something made him change his mind. The door of the cemetery was half opened. The cross had already shared into the two opposite directions as the two pieces of the door were apart.

"What the hell . . . Why the door is open?" He added with fear. The wall surrounding the cemetery was lower than the gate. As a result, someone could easily jump inside by just climbing it. Unlocking the door from the inside was not that difficult. This could work or, if someone with tiny hands, alike a child, was placing them between the gate grilles, doing it from the outside. But this time of the year and this day, this could not have happened. Nobody was there and more important, it was the cemetery. There was a reason why this place was not secured or was not well protected. There was nothing to take, it was just graves.

"Oh! Why the door is unlocked?" Nick made a question in the air once he noticed.

"Oh!" Hunch did the same exclamation as Nick, due to his surprise.

"The door should not be open now. This is not normal." Ioannis said coldly and he went near the wall, looking inside the graveyard from the top. He was seeing the graves but the light was not sufficiently to have a good look everywhere. There was only one light in the end of a long straight path made of stoned steps, which was for lighting a room under it.

"Be quiet!" Hunch gasped.

"Please! Can we go now? I do not like the idea of being here." Nick said and terror had made him surreal.

"Ok then. Come this way." Ioannis lead them from the opposite side where they have come from; the main entrance of the church's yard.

"I can't take it! I can't take it! It is too much . . ." Nick started saying, voice terrified and breaking breathes.

"We have to be quiet, in case something makes noise to be able to hear it." Hunch muttered.

"Shhh . . . I hear something." Ioannis asking for silence commanded.

"WHO IS HE?" Hunch said and he saw a figure in a dark corner.

Nick's attention moved from the open gate to the dark corner with the figure.

In a mantel, not so far form them, he was sitting silently in the corner, not moving at all. Mr. Snake, with the earphones on his ears, listening metal bands.

"What are you doing?" Hunch element of surprise acted on his face but seconds only. Then he gasped again the same question. Ioannis and Nick meet their eyes confused and Nick made the first move.

"You were here all this time? You could not answer when we were calling you?" Mr. Snake took of his earphones and made only one question.

"What did you say? Sorry but I was wearing the headphones." Calmly replied.

Hunch realized why all this time he was not responding but he still didn't get why he was just sitting there. But didn't bother asking him once he saw that even to Nick's question, he couldn't care less.

"Anyway." Mr. Snake said, the voice dead.

"I didn't find anything here." Continued his phrase and he stood up from the mantel. He was not sitting too far from the grave of the priest. The spot where they were at the present was between the front yard and the cemetery.

He approached them.

To enter the church, someone had to pass a gate larger to the one of the cemetery. And in contrary to the back gate, who was a sliding one, the front gate was a big double-gate. Passing from the gate, there was the front yard and ten meters away, was the entrance of the church. The front yard had a fountain, a garden and a well-made stoned mantel.

Long enough for thirty people to sit.

All around the church and the cemetery was an iron fence. Not a high one but neither a low one. Behind the fence, was a street, leading to another village some miles away. Someone could easily presume that this was the main street of the village. It was starting in the entrance of the village, passing through the main square, ending to the other village and in the highway.

"So . . . What do we do now?" Mr. Snake asked and looked at Ioanni.

"I do not know. Shall we go back to the house or . . . ?" He stopped his phrase for seeing Hunch examining the street.

"What is it Hunch?" Ioannis asked him.

"Nothing." His tone was clipped, avoiding Ioannis eyes.

"But you seem like you have seen a ghost. What is it?" Nick worried about his mental condition asked. Hunch stammered something and he let out a shaky breath.

"Will you tell us for God's sake!?" Ioannis yelled at him.

"I think I saw something, or someone behind the fence!" replied unease.

"He lost it guys. Just look at his face. He . . ." Mr. Snake said simple but once he saw what Hunch was talking about, lost his voice.

"What, who is he!" Nick said and his fear made him to say those words loud.

Something which looked like a man was standing behind the fence, staring at them.

The lights around the fence glimmered at the periphery of their vision. Whatever that thing was, it was scanning them quickly as none of them could say something.

They all have stayed flabbergasted and they didn't dare to say a word. The man looking thing did a movement. It started running on their direction. It was running really fast as it was flying. It passed in front of them, always behind the fence and disappeared into darkness.

"WHAT THE FUCK IS THAT!" WHO IS HE?" Hunch petrified screamed with all his power.

"WHAT IS GOING ON!?" Nick followed with screams.

"This cannot be happening!" Ioannis said and he lost his senses as he saw the thing disappearing into darkness. It was like he was wounded only by seeing it.

"It is . . . IT IS FLYING!" Mr. Snake said with an unbreakable voice.

Their voices rasped. They were already exhausted and trebling from fear and shock. They were tired from the trip and this night wasn't helping in the minimum their resting. After several second that the thing dismissed, they all tried to come in their common senses.

The wind was blowing harshly and somehow you could still hear the sounds of dogs barking. Peace touched their hearts once they realized that whatever that thing was, now it had gone. They found a moment, that moment, to analyze the situation and come up with a plan. As far as now, everything which was happening was against them. Ioannis, cutting rides in circles, began organizing his head for a plan.

"Listen! What we saw I am very afraid that was no human. I believe that, for some unexplained . . ." he stopped, having a look at the others and he continued.

"Not unexpected actually reason . . . ." And before he continues any further, Nick interrupted.

"What do you mean when you are saying "not unexpected"? You were ready to say unexplained, why did you change it?" Nick hissed and looked at him appraisingly.

"I am not the one who was talking all day about the legend of some shepherd if I remember correctly! Was I? Was I not the one telling you that I didn't like the whole story of the God damn legend?" he broke off, staggering back.

"You mean that this flying thing was the same thing that your father had seen, years ago? The shepherd?" Nick asked him, finding hard to believe it but without taking his eyes off him.

"I can't be sure. I have never seen it myself all these years. Only recently I learned about that and ever since, I was not talking about it. But I presume, yes. This is the SPEPHERD which my father was talking about." His mind still juggling the vision of its figure.

"And now what does it want? Do you think that he or it, whatever, is responsible for what is happening today?" Mr. Snake asked him, waiting for his answer.

"I do not know guys. I really have no clue. But I do have an idea." Ioannis brought in light a proposal.

"Let us hear it." Nick said. However, whereas they were all participating in all this, Hunch was doing nothing. Usually, he should be the one with the questions and the surprised expressions. But no, this time was different. He was barely listening, unable to partake in the conversation. Ioannis noticed that before he went on with his plan and wondered how that could be possible. So he made a pause on explain what he had in mind and turned to Hunch.

"Will you please tell me why you are not interested on my plan?" he asked him irritated.

"Well . . . I just do not believe in what you are saying. I still believe that this is all a prank." Hunch said but he was hesitating for fear of Ioannis reaction. He was uncertain of the figure. He didn't want to trust a lie. But he was right of Ioannis reaction.

Ioannis shook his fist and he let a long breath come out of his lungs.

"Listen, Hunch! Whether you believe that all this is a prank or not, I have something to tell you. WE DO NOT GIVE A SHIT OF WHAT YOU BELIEVE! Countless times you proved us that you are a major idiot. This time, you are doing it again. Will you ever learn from your mistakes? Will you!" He yelled at him with hate. Ioannis words had so much dark oomph coming out from his mouth, which Hunch couldn't even look at him in the eyes. He had bent his head and he, as a young child who had just done something bad, was looking on the ground. He was reacting like this every time he was feeling anger against him.

"And now that we took care of the idiot of the party, let's go back to my idea." Ioannis snapped. Mr. Snake and Nick were waiting patiently.

"First of all. Nick with Hunch will return to the kinder garden to check if Tony has returned. If not, come back here quickly and report it. Mr. Snake and I will stay here to wait for you. It has light here and it is safe for now. As I want to believe, if this was the ghost of the shepherd, I want to believe that it will not come anywhere near churches ground that is why it remained behind the fence and didn't enter inside."

"But why do we have to go?" Nick broke in.

"Yes! Why do we have to do it?" Hunch repeated frowning.

"Because, Hunch, you do not believe. So you are going. And I do not want to come along with you because right now I want to beat you. So it is Nick or Mr. Snake. If you want take Mr. Snake with you." He teased.

"I do not see the need of separating again . . ." Hunch mumbled.

"Go to hell! Just go to the kinder garden with Nick. Otherwise I will start running far away from here and then I want to see what the three of you will do without me!" he threatened him, his words strong and vile.

"HUNCH! DO AS HE SAYS!" Mr. Snake yelling the words, added in the controversial conversation.

"Let's go." Nick said and he started walking outside of the church. Hunch asked him to wait but without having any other options left, feeling as an intruder, he went with him. For a lunatic instant, he thought that it could be more suitable, he to run and leave them. His brain had started dropping in insanity.

The village at night was even more thrilling than the day. Years ago, the village used to be inhabited by entire families and people who were working there. It had a school, and its own mayor. Unfortunately since the years entering the wheel of time, the children grow up and one by one, left the village. Only few people remained but without families, and with no other choice since the life had started fainting away, they started leaving as well. None would like to stay in a village where was forgotten from the God. Without children, the school closed. When the children left, some took along and their parents. They could not let them all alone. So without people, the mayor quitted. Without mayor, the village started disappearing from the civilized world. Without people to know about its existence and make visits or trade, the village just depopulated and got forgotten.

Of course, as a holiday destination, this village still had its beauties. Some have also returned and had their houses rebuild, for the use of the vacations time only. Some others were coming just to relax in a place far away from city. The location was not bad, since it needed two hours to travel from Athens there. Others, wanted to pay a visit at the place where all their childish memories coming from, even if their houses were not in the best of the conditions to stay in.

Ioannis, Tony and their friends have come only for one reason. They wanted to have fun and enjoy four days of unlimited fun. Their trip, had nothing to do with past memories or nostalgia about the village.

***** ***** ***** ***** ***** ***** ***** ***** *****

"What is that noise that does SH SH SH!?" Ioannis scared turned his head on the direction of the priest's grave. They were walking in the yard when he heard that weird noise coming from the grave.

"I think that is an owl. I do not know how they do the sound but if it is not that, what else can be?" Mr. Snake inspired an excellent enquiry.

"My friend, I think I am losing it. First, the thing that we saw disappeared! How did that happened? I mean, you know. And now that sound? It is creepy around here. You can't disagree." He looked at him abruptly.

"Of course and I agree. If I was alone, I would not even dare to come here, especially at night." He said and he shivered.

Not far from the church, Nick and Hunch without losing time, have been to the kinder garden. The place seemed even creepier now that it was only the two of them, alone there. The barking curiously was never stopping and the wind sometimes was going stronger, making them have a chill on their spines, some other times, it was just as warm as a normal summer windy. The moon was lighting beautifully in the sky and in any other case but this one which was a night full of unforeseen shocks, it would be great for a walk.

Nick went near the edge of the fence of the kinder garden but he didn't even consider the fact of going down.

Hunch went next to him and helped him locate Tony. They waited, shadow-thin, until their eyes accustomed themselves to the dark scene down on the kinder garden. Eventually they were able to grasp one thing and only. Tony surely was not there. He hasn't returned and he was not waiting for them in the bench.

"And now what do we do?" Hunch sighed.

"Does it look like to you that I know? I am not the head here. Ioannis said to both of us to see if he had returned, thing that of course hasn't done." He provided.

"But shall we wait here or not?" asked, already certain of the reply.

"He is not here. That means that something bad happened at him. He cannot be taking part on a prank. I mean, think of it. Jim disappeared. I accept that he could make out a plan to scare us or to make us worry like idiots. And then Void too. Let's say that somehow the two of them have spoken and under some deviled conspiracy, they collaborated to this so called "bad joke". Because if it was, it would be a bad joke . . ." Hunch cut him off.

"Yes but . . ." Hunch tried to say, but due to his slow way of speaking, he could not make it before Nick interrupt him.

"There is no but Hunch. As far as now, I could believe that this was a prank. But Tony? Tony does not do this kind of things. So I no longer believe that this is some sort of prank and I hope that you will stop believing it as well. You saw that thing that flew and disappeared into nowhere? Did you see that?" he asked him shuttered.

"I agree with you. I was having some doubts but now that you told me this, it all makes sense. If you collect all the pieces of a puzzle, then you realize that WE are the ones doing the mistake." Hunch retorted.

Nick looked at him funnily but he did not let him see that. The serious way he was talking, was just not easily for someone like Nick, knowing Hunch, to get used to it.

"So we agree that we are having an emergency situation here and that we should act before something else happen to us too."

"I agree my friend! But let me also say this to you. I am stupid that I believed that this was a prank. Ioannis was right after all. Sometimes I do not know how to accept my mistakes." He apologized.

Since there was nothing else for them to do there, they start walking back to the church.

Breathing heavily and running like a fugitive, Ioannis appeared before they make it to the church. He coughed several times and he was trying to find his breath, taking big and long, but still fast breaths in and out of his lungs.

"Mr. Snake!" his face was pale and he coughed once again.

"Come with me! Come fast!" he said hoaxing and he started directing back at the church.

"How did you lose him from your sight? How?" Hunch asked astounded.

"I . . ." but he could still not talk, not having regain his breath back.

"Ioanni, how . . ." Nick was about to ask him but Ioannis got the strength to start talking again.

"Listen. We, or at least, I, heard an odd noise from inside the graveyard. Weird things are happening; I do not know what is going on here. The graves are grinding! He told me that he wanted to go and check. I am not sure, he may have heard the sounds, and he may have not. The result is that he went on the graveyard. I told him that it was insane and especially after today's nuttiness. He did not listen. He said he had the flash light and that was it."

"May I ask something?" Nick wanted to say something but Hunch overtook him.

"Is this the second advent of Christ? What is it?" hunch holding his right arm on his heart said.

"Wait a second." Nick pleaded him but he had no stop now.

"What the hell? All the dead ones are resurrecting?" Hunch ranted.

"I cannot believe it." Nick said terrified.

"Why did you lose Mr. Snake from your sight?" Hunch asked Ioanni, accusing him for his disappearance. He made an aggressive move, albeit weakly, toward Ioanni.

"Just a second." Nick tried to say again but this time Ioannis did not let him.

"Are you serious? You wanted me to go to the GRAVEYARD?" He scold at Hunch seeing him hostile. There was no way, even under these circumstances, to let Hunch play the bully.

Hunch felt the threat and did a step back.

"Wait a second, wait a second. It is my turn." Nick said anxiously, thing that made them both stop talking. And he continued.

"The guy on the black, do you realize that what we saw it is out of the ordinary?" Nick's voice was causing them more fear as they already had.

"That's what I am saying!" Ioannis said and at the same time, Hunch said as well.

"It scared me so much when I saw it! It seemed like he was wearing a hood and it was running like that!" Hunch nervously told them and began copying the way the man or the thing they have saw, was running.

"That is what I am trying to tell you!" Nick and Hunch looked at Ioanni with horror. They wanted to learn what happened but they were also scared to hear it.

"After he went to the graveyard, I saw something moving near him. That thing was there! One second Mr. Snake was there and the other second . . . Vanished!" his voice was running with extremely fast rhythms. They knew that, this night, something was wrong. Something was happening and they were feeling it to their bones. The adrenaline was in the skies.

"As fast as Mr. Snake disappeared, I came to find you. Follow me." Ioannis said, wanting them to follow him back to the graveyard.

"Forgive me." Very quietly, so quietly hunch said, in fact that Ioannis was not sure whether the words were the words he whispered or not.

Nick found himself, looking at Hunch. He felt a twinge of worry.

"I . . . I do not think that going back at the cemetery is a good idea Ioanni. I told you, I cannot do that!" said with a trembling voice.

"I agree. At devils nest, you shall not go." Hunch was trying to tell them but Ioannis was still talking, making his voice not audible.

"So what shall we do?" Ioannis asked Nick and his tone was flat.

"Can I stay here and wait for you?" staying at the church's gate, he suggested.

"Do don't even fathom to leave this spot!" Ioannis protecting him said. Everything around them was swallowing by darkness. Clouds covered the moon and its light, diminished.

"We should avoid going on Devil's nest." Hunch said this time and his voice was heard. Ioannis did not lose his time and he gave him an impact answer.

"But Mr. Snake did! We must go and find him. What if something happens to him? It is not something that we can't worry anymore. It is real!"

There was a pause for a while. They stood immobile, listening, waiting. Hunch's face was terrified.

"Do you hear the dogs? Do you hear it? They are barking like possessed." said, whispering, mouth crammed.

"I know that before I wanted to save him but I cannot do that. I am scared and I declare it. In the cemetery I cannot go." Nick went on sadly.

Ioannis shook his head disappointed and he passed from the gate. He was going to the graveyard. Nick and Hunch felt that by separating from him, could cause another disappearance.

His, or worse, theirs!

Not having lots of options left and since Ioannis knew the village and they needed him, they went on with him but they were still trying to convince him not to.

"I believe this is your mistake. You left him go on his own down there." Hunch accused Ioanni. This was the second time he have found courage to raise his head against him. Hearing that, Ioannis stopped and countered him.

"HE WENT ON HIS OWN! I COULD NOT STOP HIM!" Said yelling but the tone was low. He didn't want to shout too loud, he was afraid that someone other than them could hear him.

As entered the yard, Ioannis continue walking alone, he realized that the two of them were not following him.

He cried.

"Please, come with me to find him!"

"Why do I have to stay alone? Do you want something to happen to me?" Nick scowled.

"No one told you to stay here. You want to! We must go and find Mr. Snake. We must!" and his voice changed, being solid again.

"If we are three, we have better chances. I agree! Let's go!" Hunch asserted, his spirit became strong again.

They started walking again.

"At least, we will risk our lives to find a friend!" Hunch said poetically.

Nick cowardice, cautiously, having eyes everywhere, not sure whether to stay alone or to follow, kept going further inside to the yard. They were almost near the spot that they were standing when the incident with the man-thing happened.

"Here! Here!" Hunch said and his voice became cold. He was pointing behind the fence, where it had precisely appeared.

"This thing . . . It was flying! Let's do not talk about it. Where did it go? There is nowhere to run to! How did it disappear?" Ioannis retorted bitterly.

"There was nowhere to run, indeed! Where did it go?" Hunch repeated Ioannis last words with great query. All this conversation was becoming under the note of frightened voices.

Even if they wanted to talk normal, they could not make it. They were talking silently, almost like whispering and their voices were soaked in dread.

"It disappeared before our own eyes. It is very odd." Ioannis said to Hunch. Trying perhaps, to convince him even more that what they had testified was not human.

Hunch frowned.

Ioannis could not keep up with his breath. He was so over nervous, that he had to talk so as to do not lose it from his fear.

"And, and when I was with Mr. Snake here earlier, the grave of this priest, started grinding." And he showed them the eerily grave.

Nick shuddered.

They were now standing in front of the graveyards gate. They were gazing at it stunned. Had it truly been as difficult for three males as them, not being able to hold their fear?

"Mr. Snake went in there alone!" and jabbed a finger in the cemetery's direction.

"To begin with, why is the gate open?" Nick said and he shuddered once more to the dark thoughts which were passing through his mind.

"Yes! Why?" Hunch made the same question and all his senses flooded.

"I do not know . . ." Ioannis gave an unsure answer and he exhaled.

"Nothing?" Nick's tone was clipped, he snapped. He was trying to search Ioannis face for an answer but he could not see anything apart from trashes of fear and disbelief.

Hunch said with his voice low profiled.

"We should be really quite now, for concentrating to outer noises." He was trying to hear any possible sound around the cemetery. If someone was there, he wanted to know.

He went closer to the gate and he passed in. Nick and Ioannis copied him. They were now one step in the graveyard.

"I do not want to be here right now." Ioannis note on his voice testified his hesitation on going any further on a place as eerie as the cemetery.

"I do not feel well! I feel something on my stomach." Nick said and his voice was trembling, eager. He touched with both hands his stomach and he looked like sick. For a moment, his gyrating head lost control, his ears whined, his eyes blurred. Panic crawled up from his bowels, ranking the tissue of his gut and his stomach as he entered.

"I feel the same as you Nick, like a bond in my stomach that I can't get rid of it." Ioannis conceded.

They were both too scared. The longest they were staying there the strongest the fear was becoming. It was making them sick. They could not handle it easily.

"The idea of the graveyard alone makes your senses to react. Let alone now that we are literally here." Hunch added and his voice sounded funny.

A noise coming from the other side of the graveyard made Hunch stop talking and listen carefully the atmosphere.

"Shut up!" he exclaimed.

"Is this down there a grave or my eyes are making tricks?" Ioannis said, talking about an old grave on the right, near the fence. It had an aged tree sprouted on its top and it looked like a terrible skinny freaky person.

The cemetery wasn't too big but, a cemetery is always a place that causes fear, and even more when its night. It had seven lines of twelve graves on the right and another seven on the left. It was gradually going down and in the end, there was a room with the only light in the cemetery, above it. And that one light was not even powerful enough to light properly. It could barely illuminate the room under it.

There was no made path on that spot. Everything was pure dust and stones.

There was also another room not too far away from the room with the light. This room was smaller and it was surrounded by plants. The door was drawn between them and it was difficult to access it since the path to the door was blocked by spiny plants.

DOUUUUUUN!!!!

"What, what . . . ? Did you hear that?" a strong sound of something alike bell, echoed and re-echoed while they were waiting on the gate. Hunch eyes staring, face frozen mask of dread.

He raised his hand and with his index finger he pointed unspecified.

"Please let's leave from here!" Nick tried to speak the words aloud but something kept him from it.

"Mr. Snake?" Ioannis asked with loud voice but he felt a churning coldness in his stomach.

There was silence for a second.

"What is that? What the fuck is that?!!!" Nick's voice was blurring of terror. Ioannis eyed him guardedly. He haven't seen anything but being cautious, he starting running behind Nick, who had put his legs on his back and he had gone outside of the graveyard.

"Keep your voices down!" Hunch unstrung told them. He had remained inside. The two of them, Ioannis and Nick, were watching the graveyard from behind the stoned wall which was protecting it.

"Ioanni!" Nick said and he looked around like a cornered animal.

"What is it, you dumbass?" He postulated him but Nick gave him no answer.

Again there was a rapid time of peace. Hunch started making sounds of apprehension in his throat.

"There is something stirring down there!"

"I cannot see something. Where is it?" Ioannis whined.

Hunch was losing his words. He wanted to say something but letters only were dropping off his mouth.

"It is . . . It is moving? What is it?" he finally made to spell.

Ioannis moved his head in trepidation, left and right, without knowing where to put his eyes on. Until he finally found it.

"I can see it!" a petrified voice sounded and he rubbed his eyes due to surprise, not being able to tell if this was a human person or not.

"I can see it too! There! There it is." Hunch was unsteady and he still had his finger on the air, raised, showing at the things direction.

Under the small light of the room, where people used for putting bones or remains, a dark figure was transpiring. It was not clear but it was a figure of something alive. Tall and skinny, not able to tell precise characteristics, but it was something anomalous.

"Don't shout! Let's run away from this place now that we can!" Nick sounded as the most scared of all.

But Ioannis could not believe that easily what he was seeing. Even if he believed on supernatural, this time had to be absolutely certain.

He yelled and he enquired.

"Is anybody there?

"It is . . . An Alien!" Hunch said and he believed it.

Ioannis gave him an irresolute look but Hunch continued.

"Alien!"

Ioannis saw his friend was acting under excitement but he dint want to spoil his moment. One way or another, it is not every day who someone's living a strong emotion alike this one.

"Ioanni come back here to have a closer look." Hunch told him calmly.

"Why did you let Mr. Snake go in there?" Nick complained.

Hunch was also outside now. Outside of the graveyard. Ioannis came closer to him with small steps.

"Calm and cool. I can still see it!" Hunch said.

"What calm and cool?" Nick questioned.

"THERE! THERE!" Hunch's voice was playing in ten different frequencies.

Nick could not stay calm among all this mess. His blood was bouncing up and down but even like that, he was remaining silent, observing.

"It is moving, heading to the door of the room. It is an alien!"

"Who is there?" Ioannis shouted.

No answer.

"We should not stay here any longer! It is high time we left the cemetery. We are going back home now!" Ioannis commanded.

"But I can still see it! It is far from us!" Hunch bursting with excitement said.

"There is a car coming . . ." Nick said and he sounded like hypnotized. He was still like a rock, not having the power to accept all this.

"We are going! I don't hear a word!" Ioannis kept saying to Hunch.

"No. Wait, give me a second."

"What if this is the ghost?"

"That thing . . . . this is not human!" Hunch said resentfully.

"That is what my father had in all probability seen that time!" Ioannis was trying to make Hunch understand that this was no time for games. They had to consider this as an important incident and act carefully.

Nick did more steps behind and droning said.

"Can we please go back at the house?" a tear almost dropped from his eyes.

"If you are enjoying it that much Hunch, you can stay here." He exchanged a look with Nick. He suddenly closed the gate of the graveyard and with Nick, started running.

No sooner than they began to run, Hunch realized he had to do the same, otherwise he would have left all alone in the cemetery, close to that unidentified thing.

He felt that he was staying behind and he tried to catch up with the others. He shouted at them to slow down. His movements were slower than his friends because he was not really happy to leave the cemetery. Even though he was scared, he needed to know what that thing was.

Due to all this fused excitement he had felt, he had a hard time breathing easily. Swallowing fast, he managed to say.

"Do not run! That is how we lose each other." His voice had a panicked note.

Nick paused for a second and he answered him apprehensively.

"But is it possible to do not run in situations like these?"

"No!" Ioannis said instead of Hunch, as if the question were utterly ridiculous.

Hunch tried to found his breathing back. He wanted to say something in advance but Ioannis talked faster.

"Before that you went to the kinder garden, did you find my brother?"

"No! He was not there!" Nick saddened answered him.

"I see . . . We have to return now. I think that we are doing one mistake after another." And his tone was strict.

"Finally. A wise decision." Hunch struggled to say after managing his breathing. He wanted to examine the thing but he also knew they had to act as adults and walk away from there. His fear was, to separate again. That was what Ioannis meant as repetition of the same mistakes.

Without second thoughts, they start heading back.

"We asked "who is there". And we got no answer. I am positive, a hundred percent that there was something there, moving. A human, I doubt. It was an alien!" Hunch was saying all over, again and again, repeating his self.

Since they arrived at the churches' gate, hunch paused. Something made him wonder and made a question.

"Why is the door open?"

"I left it from before. We are not going from the way we came. We will use a different itinerary this time." Ioannis answered his question, also adding additional information.

"You haven't closed it? Are you not mistaking?" he asked him for one more time.

"I forgot to do it. Or better, I saw no point back then on closing it. Satisfied?" irritated answered Hunch's stupid questions.

"Hold your selves for a second." Hunch hinted. Both Nick and Ioannis stared at him.

"Tony?" he shouted, having his eyes turned on the kinder garden.

A brief moment of silence.

"He is not here." Stated and nodded them to walk away.

***** ***** ***** ***** ***** ***** ***** ***** *****

The root they have chosen to follow now, it was different than the other. Instead of passing from the center of the village, they were doing a circle all-around of it. Passing in front of some over and done farms, ending at their house. It was harder to walk since it was not a fixed road and not only that but, it was an uphill. A long, straight all the way until the farms, uphill.

"I believe that it is saver to follow this road. I don't feel well, passing in front of the peasants again. Let alone to tell them what happened at the graveyard." Ioannis proclaimed.

The uphill, was making them talk slower than their normal tones, because it was making it difficult for them to walk and breath and talk, all together at the same time. Their lungs could not handle the adrenaline flowing in their veins mixed with the all day's exhaustion. They needed rest and recovery for the heart to start sending proper amount of blood to the body again. For now, they were at their limits, may have already surpass them.

"If they are missing for real, then I am going to call the police. But it is not the time yet to do it. I need to junction it with something else." Ioannis confessed.

"With what?" Nick said, looking surprised.

"With everything that happened in the house." He revealed.

Hunch followed Ioannis intuition without having any second thoughts. He also believed that whatever happened in the graveyard had a common source with whatever had happened back in the house.

Although, his mood changed. "I can't believe it! We saw . . . with our own eyes something like a ghost!" and a big smile appeared on his face.

Nick shared a look with Ioanni.

"It was like a ghost!" he repeated laughing. He put his hand to hide the smile on his face. He was so surprised and eager that he could not be serious.

"Just a second. And we are leaving Mr. Snake here?" Nick through disappointment said.

"Mr. Snake who? Did you see any Mr. Snake there?" Ioannis groaned. Leaving someone behind was not a good sensation but they could not do otherwise. They should look for their own lives. They were only teenagers after all who wanted to have a funny weekend.

He didn't like the fact that they have left only three but he could not return back to search for someone who wasn't even sure if he was there anymore.

And even so, even if Mr. Snake was still there, the figure they have seen, ghost or alien, was certainly there. Roaming around, causing fear to anyone who would like to try and go near it. He was still feeling the chilling on his spine.

"I was . . . I was ready to go in there and touch the ghost!" Hunch amused announced.

"This was the ghost that my father had seen, unquestionable. The ghost of the shepherd! I don't know why now, but it is no good that appeared today. No good at all." Ioannis disclosed.

"You suggest that we will be in trouble? That is why all this happening? Because of the legend and its shepherd?" Nick asked him horrified.

Ioannis nodded his head without conviction. This it was only a theory. Maybe there was something else they haven't noticed or seen. Something that they were missing. Or maybe it was all part of something greater than a legend.

He began coughing as they were almost closing near a turn. After this turn, the road was becoming straight again without any further uphill and on its end was their house. The fatigue on his body was making him sick.

"And I didn't use to believe on ghosts . . ." Nick muttered.

"Ha . . . It is high time you believed my friend!" Hunch declared. His passivity in his face of this new horror broke Nick. Hunch was responding as though this horror were the most natural sigh in the world.

"I was always having the conviction, that all those stories were crap." Nick's note was different.

"I think I will be sick soon. I hate it. I over did it today and my body could not take anymore." Ioannis was cursing everything around him. One of the few things he really hated was to be sick. He was too proud to get sick and he was trying every day to do not do useless things that will hurt his internal organization.

He coughed few more times.

"We lost the mobiles! The mobiles! We do not have something to communicate with!" Hunch proclaimed. But as he was talking, Ioannis cut him off.

His hands clenched into fists.

"Your main problem is the lost mobiles Hunch? We have lost four of our friends and this is your only concern? I lost a brother and a cousin stupid HUNCHBACK!" he said in an all-out anger attack.

Nick was looking around for any random actions the ghost could do. Luckily, he had a good vision from the spot they were. Being on a high ground, they could see the church better. The kinder garden was also accessible to see. Of course due to the night sky, he could not see if there was a movement but he could tell if someone was at least after them.

From the other side of the road, there was an open farm with no more than ten trees. So whatever was after them, if it was trying anything against them, they could at least be prepared this time. They were in an open area and they could see everything!

As the other two, fighting about the importance of the missing things, he touched his heart. He felt it beating in such fast beats who could tell that he was in tension. He wiped his sweaty palms on his trouser. Was it horror? Was it because they were walking fast to get away from the church? One thing was certain, Nick had a strange face. A face that could only be caused by fear.

He caught Hunch's hand while he was trying to explain to Ioanni that under no account he meant that the disappearance of his friends was not important. He grabbed it and he placed it over his heart.

"Can you feel it?" he asked him.

Hunch was at a standstill. He popped his eyes out of his skull.

"You are dead! You are a living dead right now." He retorted.

Ioannis accidently haven't realized that they have stayed behind as he was walking faster than them, without taking notices behind him. He saw they were not following him and he went back to make them do faster. Nick proposed him to put his hand in his heart too, as if to feel his heart beats. Ioannis did put his hand on Nick's heart and he felt the crazy heart rate it was beating.

Breathless as he was, Ioannis told him.

"It is not only you my friend. Mine is like this as well."

"Mine is a bit too." Hunch said joyfully. He was enjoying the fact that his fearless friends were scared but he also wanted to be, even in this situation, a part of the team.

So he said that, even if his heart was beating ordinarily, because he wanted to not be any different than them. He didn't want to make them think that he was above them, playing it cool and fearless.

Finally they have reached the pick of the road. This was the end of the uphill, straight path they have chosen. The road was continuing, but it was only for leading to the mountains.

Away from the village.

They turned right and they continued straight ahead to the house. There were plenty of lights on the side of this road fact that was making it safer. The house from there was not far. It was just another straightforward way.

"Can you tell me again, why we chose this road?" Hunch questioned.

Ioannis shook his head.

Although, he replied evenly.

"Because, this is like a short cut and I found it safer." Hunch nodded as he understood the reason why.

Wild barking sounded in the sternness of the night.

"It was a ghost . . . It was moving. I saw it . . . we saw it. In the graveyard!" Hunch could not keep his enthusiasm. It doesn't happen every day, someone having an experience like this. Among all this fuss, he remembered that he was missing the most important element.

He had confronted another specie of life. This was something that he could never forget his entire life.

"I saw it flying the darkness and vanishing inside! This is what happened and I cannot believe!" Ioannis added crazily.

Hunch nodded again, this time to show his agreement with Ioannis words.

"From now on, I believe in ghosts!" he proudly announced.

"Ioanni I have something to tell you . . ." Nick tried to say but Hunch hadn't finished his phrase yet.

"And in Aliens." He added with the same proud tone.

"You are right. I would be at the same state as you are, if I haven't heard the story from my father. I always believed him and I never doubted he was telling me the truth. For me, this was more of a shock because of the flying and disappearing thing. But I can see now why you feel this thrilled. For you and Nick, this was something I do not expect you to accept, even if you have already testified it with your own eyes. But now, it happened and whatever you believe, there is no other choice but to accept the fact that this happened."

"That's right!" Hunch agreed.

"I accept it!"

The barking became louder and because they were hearing it closer to them, they froze. After everything they have passed this night, having a mad dog coming after them, would be the cherry on the pie.

"We must hurry and return home now!" Ioannis didn't forestall to finish his phrase and Nick jumped into his talking.

"I believe that there is not only one shepherd!"

This new clue that he brought into light, made the atmosphere around them foggier.

"How come and you came up with this theory?" Ioannis asked him and he narrowed his eyes. He was ready to listen anything from Nick.

"Think a bit. We send Tony to check at the house and at the same time not only him but Mr. Snake as well, went to check on the graveyard for something that you have seen. It could not possible be in two different places at the same time! Or it could?" Nick out of fear expressed another shocking revelation.

Was the shepherd only one ghost or there were more than one?

And even worse than that.

Had it some short of mystical powers? Could it do things out of the ordinary since it was not a human? Like being in two different places at the same time, or appearing and disappearing from one place to another without space consequences?

These questions were now on top of everything. If it was that they were against an unknown enemy like a ghost with these powers, then they were in even more critical danger than they already were.

"I warned you to do not let Tony go alone to the house. This was a BIG mistake!" Hunch alleged upset.

"I could not imagine that all this could happen tonight. I had no reason to believe that a ghost could be after us." Ioannis explained him serenely.

"Maybe I should go and . . . ."

"No! If you go I will beat you to death!" Ioannis warn Nick, who was ready to volunteer and go ask for help.

"It is not the time yet. Even if all this have happened, we still need to go at home. We must be truly convinced that they are missing before we request help. And when I mean missing, I really mean missing." Ioannis voice was insubstantial, like a foreign station found on a radio, words from some unfixable place.

"Mistake number one: We let Tony to come at the house alone." Hunch began saying but he was cut off.

"This is a common mistake that happens in all the horror movies. And we are proud that we are experts on Horror movies." Ioannis marked.

"True." Hunch agreed.

Then he continued.

"Mistake number two: You lost eye contact with Mr. Snake."

"A shouting star?" Ioannis added, referring to the sky.

"That is another omen!" troubled reported.

"We are indeed stupid . . . Since morning we had so many omens and we defined them all . . . It is our fault." Nick's eyes founded staring the ground.

Hunch pleaded them to stop talking. He had heard a noise. Something was weird around there. Something was happening near them. The barking dogs were close. Nevertheless, there was something scarier than that.

Hunch heard the noise again; he also saw a shadow coming closer to them.

The shadow of a BEAST!

***** ***** ***** ***** ***** ***** ***** ***** *****

A cat jumped on their way and Hunch's heart almost stopped. His entire body made on step back and pissed off he yelled.

"Go to hell cat! I almost lost my life with you!" The cat used up no more than five seconds gawking at them, until it started running again.

The unexpected happenings were following one after another. A dog, a big white guardian dog, almost as tall as a person, some steps before they arrive at its spot, it began barking. This barking became wilder and put them under thoughts, whether they should pass now from there or not.

They knew that there was no other way they could take, because that huge aggressive dog was sitting on the middle of the only road they could take to get home.

If they wanted to take the only alternative, they had to do the round of the village and that would have caused them to lose precious time. They had to pass in front of it and to be prepared in case it attacks them.

A cool wind winded and the dog stood up. It left its spot and in a hostile way, directed on the mountains, barking, as it wanted to rummage something, or to warn its boss for an intruder.

"This is out of the sphere of ordinary. The dogs cannot be barking all night!" Hunch said.

"I can't agree more with you." Ioannis finished quietly.

"They are having their instincts more developed than us. I mean humans. Whatever it makes the bark last like this, it has to be somewhat terrifying." Nick declared.

After an insignificant tick without talking, Nick asked Ioanni what he had to do. He never got the chance to get his answer.

"Someone is inside the house, this is unquestionable." Hunch observed archly even though they haven't been there yet.

Almost being to the house next of theirs, Hunch made a move. He spoke out a brief word, hard to describe which word that was, and he ran. Targeting the house.

"Come back here yaro!" Ioannis called him and he used another Japanese word, for the word bastard.

"We are going to lose him!" Nick screamed.

They followed him in the night, under indescribably tiredness. Hunch had no reason to start running out of the blue. Once again, the feeling of fear, which had never left but had only been on the back burner, came back to all it is gravitas.

Apparently, another barking was sounding from the way Hunch had chosen to run. A barking louder than this of the big white dog.

"Hunch come back! You will become food for the dogs!" Ioannis pleaded him to return or at least to wait for them to catch up.

He obeyed.

"Why you make it a big deal? I am tired on wasting more time in stupid things. We should be home by now and instead of that, we are walking like zombies and . . ." before he said more, he bit it back. He saw Ioannis rage at his eyes and found it clever to do not continue.

"Next time you will do that, do not matter the shepherd. The one who is going to kill you it is ME!" Ioannis gave him a last piece of advice. He said it in a way, that sounded like a warning though.

Stupid actions had no end among them and it was only natural, him to get mad. The night was still going on and their only proof of their friend's disappearance was a legend. If things were on the edge, they had no confirmations to prove their innocence.

Four people on a small village gone missing, the way the situation was right now, everything was against them. Luckily the barking was coming from the road of the root they haven't followed.

"Do not be afraid. I knew that there was no dog here. After all, if you believe that we will not have proofs to show to the police, you have us." Hunch said to help him.

"I am not afraid of the police, I want to find my friends and I do not give a damn about what the police will think." Nick said mildly.

"I am worried about the police Hunch, because even if you are here, they can still accuse the three of us. We need to find proofs that the ghost-shepherd is real and it took them. Should they are not at home now, of course." Ioannis sneered.

It was nearly eleven o'clock when Nick Ioannis and Hunch finally escaped the cavernous roads of the village, emerging near the brightness of their place of comfort.

Although, they could not fathom that the brightness they were seeking, had transformed into muddiness.

"You should know, Ioanni, that for as long as I am into your picture of vision, there is no problem." Hunch said stiffly.

Ioanni's expression tightened angrily.

"Meaning what exactly with that?"

Hunch shrugged elaborately.

This for a second only.

His eyes narrowed then, taking on a faraway look, and the pitch of his voice transmuted into dryness.

"Second fatal mistake that YOU did, you left Mr. Snake get away from your eye's range."

"It all started with the animals. That's where you have to start first." Nick told him but before he got the chance to finish, Ioannis cut him off.

"He went inside the graveyard. If it was you, would you have followed him? I don't think so. So I would appreciate it if you could stop accusing ME for his stupidity. The ghost flew! There was nothing for me to do!" This was an unexpected reaction from Ioannis. Usually, having Hunch talking back on him this way, under other circumstances, he would have beaten him. But no, this night was not the same as any other. For this, things were different tonight.

Although he made a short scene, Hunch seemed to do not pay any attention on him. He and Nick were still talking. Hunch was literally "hanging" from Nick's speech.

"The crazy man, the Dracula, do you remember what he told us?"

Hunch nodded with great interest.

"We should have warned everyone since the beginning. He had something to do with all this. It was not unplanned." Nick said, words dressed with panic.

They were at their fortress. Almost at the gate of Ioannis's house. Finally their journal had reached their destination. The short destination of returning home at least.

A huge pillar of light was setting light on the road.

Color orange.

As they were walking, the sound of their steps echoing everywhere. The village had an excellent echo due to the mountains surrounding it.

Heavy, rushing steps, non-stop.

A devastated house on the right was another proof of the village's abandonees. The roof was all down and only the remains proving that in some period during time, this was an inhabited residence.

Although everyone had left and forgotten the village, Ioannis had left awakened the feeling of his house. His nostrils filled with the familiar scents of his childhood as he was passing in front of their cellar.

Endless summer nights, he had to stay there with his brother and grandparents alone. A feeling of being extremely bored, nothing to compare with the feeling of this exhilaration they were living tonight.

All of it seemed so far in the past and yet was still so familiar. Travelling back in time, this thought was always crossing his mind. But he was not sure if he would like to live all the boring parts of his life again. Perhaps his life had more mind-numbing times than amusing.

The non-stop walking clogged. The three youngsters found their selves before another great surprise.

Ioannis made the first observation, having his mouth and his eyes locked under the orange light.

"WHERE IS THE CAR!?" Hunch expressed.

"Where is the car?!" he repeated with a lower note. After that, he lost his voice.

"No way." Ioannis quivered.

Nick's eyes racked Ioanni's as he came closer at him. Ioannis run under the orange light. This was the spot where the car was supposed to be parked

"I can't believe it!" He chuckled ruefully.

"It . . . it maybe took the car as if to have enough space to put them all!" Nick grumbled.

"Now it became foggier than ever." Ioannis posted.

"How many do we miss? So many the seats on the car are." Nick flared.

"We have remained one, two, three . . ." hunch started counting. As he finished with the pointedly observation, he realized the minority.

"We have remained only three . . . ." His voice fainted slightly.

The idea which was growing in their minds, ever since they left the graveyard, it was the only boat of surviving now.

"Back to the house. There is no need to be here anymore." Ioannis commanded, his voice rushing.

"Back to the house." Nick echoed.

They were only few meters away from the gate of the yard. Only one few steps away, with the motorbike parked some centimeters further.

The gate was opened as they have left it. Ioannis made a stop before he goes in. He had to check if the motorbike was working. He had a bad feeling including the fact of the missing car.

But no, before he tries anything, as Hunch opened the gate, something more extraordinary stole his eyes.

"A candle!" Ioannis remarked.

He went closer and to his surprise, there was another one. They were three in total.

"I am losing my mind! How . . ."

"Do not make a sound! Do you hear this noise?" Hunch's voice took on a hysterical edge.

The hollow sound seemed ominous. There was an almost full moon shimmering above the mountains and dark dancing shadows passing before it.

"Please, we must go inside!" Nick cried out.

Hunch nodded and Ioannis had no objection.

"Two candle here and one had been found in the back yard." Nick had made an excellent observation and statement but it needed time for Hunch's brain to process this information.

It was there, the door, the entrance to their fortress was there. Standing so close, you could accurately smell its rotten and aged fragrance.

Would they be safe finally?

Ioannis touched the knob but once he did it, he stood immobilized.

"WHAT NOW?" Nick shot him with enragement.

"My brother has the key!" he revealed and his voice sank deep on the calmness of his thoughts.

He tried to open it, twisting the knob in the direction of the ground.

It made an unexpected sound.

"It is unlocked!!!" Ioannis voice spanned out remarkably.

Tony should have the key with him, why then the door was unlocked? What have happened inside the house?

Thoughts similar to these ones were crossing their minds. Was it beneficial after all that the door was unlocked?

Ioannis not knowing how to act decided to take the risk. The moment was crucial, for this Hunch shouted.

"Don't go in there Ioanni!

"Don't go!" Nick echoed.

Those words were enough to make him stand, have a second though.

"I don't want you to go in there because . . . where is Tony?" Where are the others?" this was the first sign of Hunch's paranoia.

"I swear, I saw him locking it with my own eyes!" Nick protested. The already heavy cloud of doubt became unaffordable.

"We do not need any more proofs I think. We have too solutions, or we go to the police or we call for help." On his panic he didn't think that they were in an almost abandoned village, where there was no police. Their only escape was the villagers.

"I will go in!" Ioannis bravely announced.

His friends, both of them, focused their attention on him.

"NO!" Nick using all his will said, trying to keep him safe.

"We are three." Ioannis answered but this is not the only thing he wanted to say. Before he finishes, Hunch yelled, cutting him off.

"No forget it!" expressed strongly. He was trying to participate on Nick's line of thoughts.

"In the beginning we were eight and now we left three." Nick mentioned, wanting to point out the fact that even if they were seven in the beginning (eight was a mistake made upon his rush), they had been reduced to three. Chances to decrease more were in elevation.

Hunch saw Ioannis hesitation and he tried to be reasonable.

"Forget about going inside. The police are our only option. And we should better go at the center and ask for help!"

None of the offers, Nick's or Hunch's, made Ioannis change his mind. He looked at them on the eyes, honest and without saying a word more, they knew that he was ready to do it. He opened the door without hesitation and he walked in.

***** ***** ***** ***** ***** ***** ***** ***** *****

He walked in a dark and hollowed place that he used to call, home. This home however, had something different tonight.

A windy aura that it never had before.

They followed him into the narrow maze corridor, a walk not quite a meter wide. Everything was different, as the house itself had transformed into a totally different formation.

No, no. This was not the safe fortress that he once was using to play with his grandparents and his brother. Something was different.

Could it be the fact he had grown up or could it be the pain he had from his loss. Not about his friends but from his ex-girlfriend.

He knew that this time, he should be thinking other things. Things like the danger which could be waiting in the next corner. He knew that and still, he could think nothing more than his past memories.

So many "adventures" happened since the last year. He had to come on this village. He had a variety of new experiences on his shoulders and he needed to be back. Back where he used to be carefree, without any problems or thoughts of an adult on his mind.

No, there was no place for fear now. Whatever was happening, it was just another experiment for him.

An experiment of life.

He raised his self and he shouted with a brash and fierce voice.

"If you are here, I WILL KILL YOU!" using the word kill, he illuminated the phrase. It made it have a more aggressive sense.

"DO YOU HEAR ME?" yelled again as he had already walked on the bedroom with the television.

"We must turn on the lights!" Hunch protested.

"Follow me, follow me. We will search the entire house!" Ioannis ordered them in a flash. He was blasting the house with reckless steps and fast peeks.

His screams comparable with the screams of a madman. He was scared and only by acting hostilely, with cursing and making noise, he could fight against the fear.

"Ioanni, you should better come here!" Nick called him.

"What is it?"

Hunch saw also what Nick wanted to saw him. He could not get to do not react.

"Why your bag is like this?!" his voice and his temper rose.

Nick's back bag was lying on the wooden floor. Opened, slightly dirty.

"My bag, which I had left . . . No, my GOD!" Nick's both hands, shielded his face. He had no will to say anything else. Ioannis started thinking what their next step should be. His thoughts didn't last long, Hunch made a proposal.

"We, we do not need more proofs." Hunch's voice trembled.

"Let's go to the café where the people are and tell them to call the police. What I don't get is the candles! Is this an alien's work? What the hell?"

"Switch off all the lights! It is a mistake to have them on." Ioannis run from one room to another to switch them off again.

Gathered in the entrance hall, Nick received a task from Ioanni.

"Nick, go the café now, ok?"

"I am going, yes!"

"Wait! There is one light left. I am going to switch it off!" Hunch pointed out and he did it.

"You switch off the light and I want to check the phone device." Ioannis enunciated.

"After the café, shall I come back here? What shall I do?" Nick asked.

"Yes, come back here but go fast. Run as you have ever run before!" he advised him.

"Why the bag was opened?" Hunch was trying to solve that mystery.

"Run, go now my friend!" Ioannis buster him to do his best.

Ready to go, just about to twist the knob of the door, a shivering voice blocked him for doing it.

"No! Why to go alone? We will go together!" Hunch said stretching out his objection.

"Really? You want us all to go out there?" Ioannis answered him with another question.

"I will be fast, I promise!" Nick added.

"Not alone!" Hunch repeated himself.

"I met some of the villagers after the basket game that we had. I will talk to them, and they will understand me I believe."

"I trust him Hunch. There is no doubt about his speed."

"No and again, no! I don't care if you are fast, we have to stick together. If you go, then we will remain only two!"

"But, it is already over. All of our friends are missing. I do not care about myself anymore . . ." his voice flushed in warmness.

"It is a GREAT mistake to separate again!"

It was true that Hunch was trying to do not repeat the same fault as before. He had sturdy motives to do not want Nick go on his own. The door was opened and Nick was standing with one leg on the yard.

"You said the same think for Tony too! Shall I repeat your words? "No he can do it. We trust him" and so on. And you see where this thinking guided us?" Hunch said upset.

"But the café is in the next corner. I do not know what will happen if he doesn't go!" Ioannis keep it up.

"Ioannis is right Hunch. I have to go. We must go and ask for help, you know that."

"No objection on that. We will go all together. Where is your problem?"

"The three of us? Do you believe that we can make it?" Nick changed his voice and sounded more frightened, his note closer to a girl's.

"Of course. The three of us together we can make it. Switch off the light on the bedroom and lets go."

"Whatever . . . I am not coming with you. Go alone, the two of you." Ioannis dissatisfied told them.

"ARE YOU INSANE? What is wrong with you?" Hunch scolded him.

"Because I have no more courage ok? If this thing attacks us on our way for help, who is going to save us?"

"The last thing that we should keep is the house. If we lost it then it is over!" Nick tried to assure Hunch that this was the dead-on action for the moment.

Hunch gave a second on himself to think and measure the situation. From one side, they were right. If that thing could get them all by once. Then it was over. But he didn't want to let Nick go alone either. Deep inside him he knew that this was the only way, to ask for help, but if Nick couldn't make it, then that automatically would mean that he would be alone with Ioanni. And things would be much more difficult if they were only the two of them.

"What I saw, it was an entity, which was flying, disappearing into darkness, took our friends and I don't know what else have done already. No mobiles, no telephone and all day, signs are appearing from everywhere. Well, yes I am scared to death and I prefer to stay here and wait for Nick than to go out there, with that thing threating my life."

Hunch realized that there was no way to make Ioanni change his mind. He was scared and he didn't seem to be interested anymore on leaving his house.

They were all confused and distracted. They could not think clear for a proper solution. Nick could not wait any more and Ioannis the same.

"This is enough! Nick, go now and ask the peasants for help!" Ioannis directed him with a fierce tone.

"Ok, if you want to do it this way, then I am coming with you!" Hunch without them to expect it announced.

Ioannis brows arched anxiously.

"And you are going to leave me alone?" with an angry but at the same time scratched voice said.

"No, no. You can't leave him now! I will run very fast and you will only slow me down. It is far better for you to stay here and wait for me to come back." Nick placed his reason why not Hunch should not come along.

Reasons reasonable enough, to make him embrace from going out in the end.

He could hear everything now. Not because he had developed senses as the dogs, not at all. It was because in this level of terror, the true atmosphere and its entourage revealed. Hunch all this time, was enjoying it, even if he had been scared several times.

This had stopped now. The wind was whipping through the few flowers which had left on the small garden of the yard. Threating to rip them up by the roots and fling them across the mountain. Even the house was shaking every now, could it be that the wind was so immerse or that Hunch had finally overtaken by the master of all emotions, fear.

"I am staying, but you have to switch on at least one light!" He countered.

"Of course!" Ioannis answered and he went to the bedroom. Straight away he returned without the light having been turned on.

His expression was a witness of his disapproval.

"I do not think that switching on the lights is a good idea." He told Hunch, his voice shook.

Nick was waiting outside on the yard for Ioanni to tell him when to go. Hunch had come in, his face anxious, his eyes beseeching him.

"If we switch them on, we are giving away our hideout. I want it to believe that we are not here. Don't you get it?" Ioannis asked his friend waiting for him to understand that he had good reason not to want to do it. In this point, he had to do everything to keep him there. Leaving him go with Nick, could be disastrous.

"Give me the flashlight. We can use candles instead. They are more suitable now. So we will not need the flashlight or the house lights." Ioannis made a small pause, stared at Nick and shouted at him.

"Are you still here!? LEAVE NOW!"

Nick nodded and he began running. He opened the gate and he closed it in fractions of seconds.

Ioannis was apprehensively searching the house for candles.

"Wait Ioanni, I don't want to lose eye contact with each other."

"With Nick you mean?" he answered to Hunch who was worried.

Hunch tried to find Nick but it was already too late.

"Nick already left. I couldn't keep my eyes on him." And he looked appall the second he got the feeling that there were only two. Now he was convinced, he had to do not lose Ioanni from his eyesight at any cost.

"I believe on Nick. He can run fast, he is going to be there in any second now. My brother . . . I don't UNDERSTAND how my brother could not make it back!" he started to rise his voice.

They moved in the kitchen. Ioannis switched on the lights. Hunch though that he heard a noise but he ignored it because he saw that it was nothing more than his mind playing tricks.

Ioannis having found nothing to use for light, switched on the kitchen's light and taking Hunch with him, closed the door of the hall. A big wooden door with a thick glass on the middle.

They decided to wait for Nick to come back in the front hall of the house, where they were all this time. Right in front of the entrance door and between the thick wooden door. The entrance hall, had a big window and they had an excellent vision of all the yard and not only. They could see from behind the yard gate, the small road where they have come from.

Now there was only one thing left for them to do. Wait for Nick to return.

Hunch broke the silence with his voice braking, as the cold ice. He was trying not to wash out his words.

"Where all of our friends gone? Jim first and then . . ." the emotion was too much for him, he forgot his words.

He went on.

"The candles! We found candles!" shouted terrorized.

"Shit . . . my heart . . . I feel it beating fast. I will have a heart attack in this point?" Ioannis said contemptuously, as he didn't want to accept the fact he was scared.

Hunch moved his hand to his forehead. A sign of great concern and disaster.

"Now I am extremely worried!" he spelled out of his mouth. All this time, he was pretending that this was an adventure. Now he knew that things have gotten wild and he had to stop acting as if they would be ok.

Because highly possible, now, things would not be able to get better. Since the beginning, he somehow had his suspicions but all became clear now. It was all real for him!

"I hate you really! You were making fun all this time and you were laughing, like all this was a joke! You mentioned the legend more than seven times! You think that you can make fun with things like that?" he asked him directly.

"No . . ." he whispered with his lips closed.

"IT WAS FLYING! Can you put this on your head?!" he frowned.

"I saw it moving, yes . . ." Hunch agreed.

"That's why you should have stopped." He scolded him.

Hunch was looking outside of the window, shrunken, waiting for Nick's advent. His mouth was literally half opened; staring like lost the hollow road from the window. His eyes fixed in the spot with the orange light, right under the electrical column.

"The dogs! Listen to them!" he pointed out with his finger raised, pointed upwards.

As horror had overhauled him, he jumped from the topic for the dogs to another. He was utterly bounded to his emotions.

He looked Ioanni with sadness on his eyes.

"Why we didn't go with him?"

"Shut up. Come to see this." He called him to go by the window which was located in the corridor of the entrance hall. They could see in the TV-bedroom from that.

Hunch approached him pale.

"Go to hell." Ioannis said with a low but contracted voice.

He continued after he did an obscene gesture at the glass of the window.

"It was my reflection on this glass. It seemed like something inhuman. Come to see it! I got scared for nothing." he invited him again after the drown emotion left him.

"Yes, yes!" Hunch totally agreed with him.

Ioannis walked impatiently upside down a couple of times.

"My skin is sparking. I cannot continue like this for any longer." Something caught his attention outside and made him exhale worse.

"Bats." He added normally.

They had everything included on this night, why not bats as well.

"What?" Hunch asked concerned

"Yes, over there. Come to see them yourself if you want."

Hunch found it worth-time-consuming to observe them from behind the window. Ioannis started walking again the hall upside down. It was not too long and at its end, was the toilet. On the other end, was another thick wooden door, hiding on the other side, Ioannis bedroom, which was the main bedroom of the house.

He went into the toile, he came out.

His footsteps clapping on the floor. His joints straggling to keep him upright. He was physically tired but due to the hyper kinetic that he had, was making it difficult for him to stay in one place only under these circumstances.

He returned back to Hunch who was still dawdle the bats and he told him with a hastening voice.

"I have to check once more whether the phone works or not."

Hunch tried to provoke him from opening the door but he was dramatically late.

The door had been already opened.

"Damn!" he alleged out of annoyance biting his lips.

The heating was first object to see. Ioannis turned his head and on his left side, was the small table with the landline phone device.

Some pencils and a not important notepad were there next to it as well. Also placed on the table, was Ioanni's portable game console.

He picked up the phone to test.

"Damn! Why it is not working?" he said frustrated and he hardened his fist. Hunch was looking also on the phone with his lost eyesight.

Ioannis tried to put it back to its place but because of the shock that was under, he missed the first two times to place it right.

He succeeded with the third one though.

"Take my psp." He requested from Hunch.

He got it on his hands and turned it on for Hunch.

"The light that this console provides, believe me, is amazing. We can use it as a flash light." He ensured him.

Both went back at the hall and closed the door behind them.

"Where is Nick? He said that he will come fast. Where the heck is he?" obviously his voice was shaking under stress. Not only he was expecting him to come back with help but now the fear of something bad may have happened at him, started to grow on his consciousness.

"Just, just, just a second." Ioannis calmed him and stopped him from being so troubled.

"If you were there, take the psp now, it's ready. If you were there, one of the villagers, and a boy was coming, telling you that his friends were kidnapped by aliens or ghosts, would you believed that?" he was waiting for his answer.

"Yes you are right. This works as a flashlight." Apart from that, Hunch seemed to have not realized that he had to answer a question. Ioannis didn't bother asking him again, once he saw that he was not functioning properly any more.

Hunch was devastated.

"Where is Tony?" He started talking to himself. Gus voice was low not because he didn't want Ioannis to hear him but because he was factually talking to himself.

Ioannis did nothing more than watching him with face tipped on him.

"Did Tony came here and took the car? But still, there is no sense on that. Why he left the door unlocked? Why he took the car? No, no. The problem is that he would never do such a thing and leave us behind. This is why this situation requires extraordinary measures." His face grew even tighter.

"I saw him locking the door!" shouted and blurted his eyes on Ioanni.

"Hm . . . Let me go to the bedroom, my bedroom and take the keys for the motorbike. We didn't check it before due to the appearance of the candles." He piped.

Hunch felt an emergency vibration to protect him.

"Not alone! Open the door and I am following you with my hand touching your shoulder. I will not lose contact no matter what!" he declared to him.

Ioannis opened the other thick door which was on the hall, the one to enter the bedroom instead of the other part of the house. He entered his bedroom. First thing he did, was to switch on the lights. Without losing time, he went on the bed where he had temporary left his luggage and he took a pair of keys which were placed next to it.

Hunch windfall, removed his hand from him and he opened the other door, the one which was connecting this room with the living room and looked inside.

Only the moonlight was bringing light onto this room. The moonlight alone and nothing else.

"I am going to try it now!" Ioannis hastening informed Hunch. His movements were fast for Hunch's dawdling ability on reacting.

"Where are you? Wait? I can't follow you in this rhythm!" Hunch voice trembled. A knot of fear congealing in his belly, no matter what, he had to stay close to him.

"Come boy! You are not losing me! I just want to do it fast. If I can start it, then we can achieve something here!" he grinned at him. Ioannis was optimistic.

Maybe there was a chance after all for them to escape this nightmare.

"Wait, wait." Hunch pleaded him.

Ioannis waited holding the door house adjust. Hunch switched off the lights they had turned on and he nodded him.

They could go now.

Passing fast from the yard into the gate and from the gate outside. The motorbike was still there. Safe and sound.

"Do you have the keys?" Hunch asked in anguish.

"Of course."

"Where is the third candle?!" Hunch to his surprise with his eyes wide open expressed.

One of the three candles was not where it should have.

"The candle? I just kicked it. I did not want it anywhere around us. Relax." Ioannis soothed him.

Hunch found it dropped a bit further than he was. They had rolled from Ioannis kick. He leaned and he scanned them.

"What are those candles for? Ksou ksou ksou!" Hunch shook his entire body and he did an old Greek custom for situation like this.

When it comes to superstitions, you can say this non-meaning word, ksou, for the evil to go away from you. It was a common custom during old ages and especially on villages.

Ioannis was on the motorbike now, he put the key on the engine and he twisted it . . .

The lights came on!

Hunch looked expectantly at his friend.

Their eyes met. Hope painted again on both faces.

But . . .

"It doesn't work . . ." Ioannis disappointed announced.

He tried again but the ignition seemed like it was having troubles. Regardless what Ioannis was trying, the motorbike apart from the lights was dead!

"Did you put the keys?" Hunch made another not logical question but Ioannis on his panic, did not even consider that it was senseless.

He answered him normally.

"The lights are on, but this doesn't mean that is working. Apparently, there is something in the engine. I cannot explain it otherwise. It refuses to catch!"

"Everything is dead!" Hunch's brows arched.

Ioannis get off the motorbike and removed the keys. He put in his pocket. He let his breath out.

"And now we now that we have nothing to run away from the village . . ." he just mentioned.

Hunch shook his head desperately.

"Even if we find a way to return to Athens, I do not want to leave my motorbike here!"

Then, they heard a hooting sound in the darkness. Distant but wild. A sudden silence had fallen between them again. They took the opportunity to look up into the darkness again, locating the moonlight beams, seeking for Nick's sign.

Their only hope was upon him now.

Ioannis was ready to return back to the house. He did not have even a drop of strength on his body. His entire world seemed like devastating and he could not do anything to stop it.

Or at least, this is how it seemed to Hunch.

"No!" Hunch raised his voice and reclaimed.

"We cannot go inside again! Where is Nick? I . . . we have to go and find him I suggest."

"He went to talk to the people who live here. It will need his time until he convinces them that there is something wrong going on. Trust me, I know better." His voice trailed off.

"But if we go there, we can convince them easier. It will be three of us."

"And if Nick returns here and doesn't find us? Then what?"

"But Nick is already there. What are you talking about?"

"Maybe something happened to him and he is trying to come here. If he comes asking for help and we are not here? This is my point."

"We should not leave the house? This is what you mean?"

"Exactly. For the moment, the problem is not Nick. But we must remain here because you never know what comes next. This is the plan and for once, we should keep up with it." Ioannis glanced toward Hunch who looked sort of confused, sort of unruffled.

The yard gate closed again and Hunch had stopped following Ioanni, paused, thinking.

"I want him, or that, to do not come inside the house. It is highly indispensable to have at least somewhere to hide. Let alone this is my house, I . . ." but Hunch cut him off.

"First thing we need to look after is our lives and then the assets." He grumbled.

Then he went on.

"After all, they can take anything they want from the house (referring to thieves in case there was no ghost, just thieves). Our lives are more valuable." Hunch wanted to say more but Ioannis interrupted, his voice clearly reflecting his doubt.

"To take things? Like steal them?"

"Yes . . ." He answered and directly he got his answer.

"To steal what? It is the shepherd." He told him. His face neutral, his eyes beseeching him.

Was it possible Hunch still had doubts about the legend of the shepherd?

Another moment of stillness, with Hunch holding the portable game console on his right hand as a flashlight and Ioannis staring at him.

"I am trying to tell you one thing here. My father had seen this exact same figure. I do not believe it myself but we have to because this is what is happening!" he pressed.

Hunch's eyes have not yet changed, remaining rationale.

"I want to stay here for the reason I expressed you earlier. We have a plan and we must follow it. If you remember, in horror movies, always happens something bad because they never stay where they should have stayed at a first place. I will not become another victim!" he fretted.

"Don't you agree?" he asked Hunch with impatience for his answer.

Hunch nodded positively.

"Excellent!" relief building. And they went inside the house again.

"We do not have any device or equipment to communicate?" Hunch's voice softly probed.

"With smoke signals. Does this works for you?" Ioannis parroted through gritted teeth, his voice taking on the mocking edge of sarcasm he always used to have.

"With a mob . . ." Hunch ready to say mobiles but out of the blue, he froze.

His finger pointing on the thick with the glass in the middle door. No, it was pointing behind the door. His eyes wide open filled with terror and his mouth hanging open tremulous. Even if he could not see through it, he felt that something in the house had changed.

It felt more alive than before. As if something behind the door was moving.

It felt wrong!

***** ***** ***** ***** ***** ***** ***** ***** *****

Once again the scene filled with a strange and ominous silence, broken only by the sound of the barking dogs outside as it slashed against their ears.

"What?" Ioannis whispered.

Hunch nodded him to listen.

"Did not tell me that you heard something? I am not going in there!" stated.

"I am still hearing it! There are noises coming behind the door. Someone is on the house . . . I think so . . . ." Hunch entrusted him.

Ioannis had nothing to say. He was biting his lips and waiting for anything to happen. Hunch began making him signs using the expressions of his face and his hands together.

"You want me to go and see from the window?" Ioannis asked with query.

The window which was on the TV-bedroom connected with the hall could help them see if there was someone in there at least. They maybe could not see the entire house from there, but the TV-bedroom was a good idea to start with.

Ioannis though to give it a shot but he had a feeling that he will get nothing. Although his feeling, he went close to the window and what happened that time, made his blood froze.

"OH OH!!! WH . . . WH . . . WHO IS HE?!" Hunch asked Ioanni, his voice unsteady, forgetting the words. Eyes wide open, terror the only expression on his face.

His dread reaction scared also Ioanni who without losing time, went near him again to see. Hunch had seen something from the long window. He had seen something outside, on the road.

"Who is he?" managed finally to say clear and he was having small jumps cause of his anxiousness.

"Who?" Ioannis replied questioning him.

'Did you see him? DID YOU SEE HIM?" his voice sharped but low at the same time.

"No, I didn't see anyone."

"I saw a person over there!" and he pointed outside of the yard, the road they have come from.

"Are you trying to scare me?" Ioannis gently asked him.

"No! I promise you; I swear to god, I saw it!" crying voice.

His hunch had grown bigger as he was hunching for having a better vision of the road.

"I saw a human person over there!" he repeated his words.

"I do not think so." Ioannis told him.

"But I did see it!" lost said.

"And why I didn't see anything?" Ioannis said with query but with a sad tone on his voice. It was possible someone to be outside of the house but he wanted, no, he needed, to see it with his own eyes this time.

Hunch mind was playing games and Ioannis knew that he was probably losing it. He had to trust him if he wanted to be safe but on the other hand, he did not know if what Hunch was seeing at this point was real or not. If what he was hearing, was within the sphere of reality or not.

Hunch was trying to conquer the panic inside him. Shifting his gaze, thinking if what he saw was nothing more than a construct of his imagination. Could not be, he knew that it was real.

It was all real!

"I am certain that I saw someone walking down the road." He frowned, his voice stable as rock.

"Are you sure that it was a human?"

Hunch nodded and he answered.

"Human, with a jean trouser and a shirt, and he was walking like this." And he copied the way he/it was moving.

"If what you saw is what I believe, it is not a human! The shepherd . . ." Ioannis paused.

"Fuck your legends!" respired.

Shifting looks everywhere, on the yard, on the street, on the house.

Ioannis opened the entrance door windfall and yelled.

"IS ANYONE THERE?"

Nothing.

"I don't see anything now. Maybe it is better this way."

"Where is Nick?" with disbelieve on his tone asked.

Ioannis got it immediately that Hunch knew that Nick was not coming back. He already had it on his mind but now he knew that Hunch had it too.

"We didn't act wisely. We should have never let him go alone! We had to go all three together." sighed heavily.

"And to tell them what?" Ioannis told him, his voice tight, eyes slightly glazed.

Hunch though for a second and he replied.

"We lost our party; we need to call the police."

"My concern, my truly concern is, that whatever we tell them, they will not believe us. They will think of it as a joke and they will not act. Instead of humiliating myself in front of them, I prefer to stay indoors and wait." Ioannis said.

Hunch breathed, the last of his air of nonchalance disappearing as he listened nervously at the darkness within Ioannis voice.

Was he right about the peasants of the village?

Even if they were trying to tell them, the only thing they could achieve could be humiliation?

"At least, is as you said my friend. You can see each other now, and never, never in horror movies when they see each other bad things happens." Ioannis assured him.

"Except of course if they appear from inside the wall . . ." also mumbled without Hunch notice it.

Keep looking through the glass; Hunch was waiting for a sign. Nick to appear and tell them the jovially news or a policeman officer or someone who could help them.

There was nothing moving outside now.

The yard was seeing emptier than usual. The absence of their friends had made it look like that and it was not only the yard. Everything was hollowed, everything even his heart.

He was missing something, his friends, people that he was carrying about and this was creating a hole inside him.

A desperate hole which was sucking life onto him.

As he was waiting for anything to happen, a voice inside him made him frown.

Turned his head on the other side to meet Ioanni, the only friend he had left now.

With a crying voice and soreness on his eyes, he spoke.

"My friend, I am truly petrified, where our friends are?" as a sign for his desperation, he touched his head and puzzled his brows.

"You really saw something? I didn't see." Ioannis asked again, not knowing what to believe anymore.

"I swear to God, a thousand percent that I saw something." Hunched whirled.

Heavy coughing coming from Ioanni disturbed the tranquility of the moment. The coughing continued for several seconds, almost like dyeing and then he stopped.

He took a breath.

The moment was uncomfortable for both of them. Ioannis was waiting for anything to happen and Hunch was magnetized on the window, looking outside.

"May I go outside? But if you saw someone or something there, I cannot hide the fact that I am afraid to go." Ioannis glanced toward Hunch.

"Where is Nick for God's sake?" Hunch indignant said.

A brief moment of silence again. But it was the old familiar silence. After all that had happened, they were in no mood for more mysteries.

A drawn-out scraping, a new sound. It was sudden, simple and dramatic.

"AAA THE CAT!" Hunch screamed out loud.

"What?"

"To hell! I got scared by this cat!"

"And it is a black one as well . . ." Ioannis added.

"Another bad omen." Hunch acknowledged.

It was too much for someone like him to take. He suddenly felt into a delirium.

"Where is the car? Why the motorbike doesn't start? Why the door on the graveyard was open? Why the graves were grinding?!"

So many unsolved mysteries and Hunch was hardly fighting now.

Ioannis had to admit that all this was driving him nuts. He knew that he didn't have lot of time until his friend lose his mind completely and start acting like mad. With no other option, Ioannis had to find a solution and fast.

He not only had to deal with an unexplained event but should he wanted to survive, keeping Hunch sane was one of the keys to achieve it.

There was a pause, and Hunch strained to hear any sound from the out world. Ioannis did the same with success.

A noise sounded.

"What is causing this sound?" Ioannis asked Hunch, not excepting an answer but simple to make it clear that he heard it.

"I . . . Yes I hear it too." Hunch followed. His heart sank for a moment as he felt nothing but the smooth surface of the night, but then, barely within reach, he found a small crack on his fear.

He regained some of his courage and helped Ioanni to open the entrance door for a check.

"Do you have any idea what that could be?" Hunch questioned by Ioanni one more time.

The door was open but they had no clue of what was coming next.

Hunch wanted to be strong. He wanted to do not let his fear overtake him again, but for this it was already too late. Even the small crack he felt for a second, languished along with his last sense of reality.

"Now what?" Ioannis wailed. He gazed Hunch but the only thing he had left now with, was an empty shell.

Hunch was no longer on his senses.

He was looking around with the portable device as a flashlight. Eyes wide opened the same as his mouth.

With a lost face, not knowing any longer if he was dreaming or if he was awake.

A second socked silence felt over the room. He was trying to think what was going to happen next. Should he go and leave Hunch and house together or shall he do otherwise?

Then Hunch spoken.

"I see something again!" his voice took on a demanding tone.

"Where?"

"Oh?! It disappeared!" his puzzled frown deeper.

"Again?" said not being able to believe him this time.

"I . . . It was over there!" he stammered.

"I don't know . . ." Ioannis looked at him with disbelieve.

Hunch illusions continued again, twice in a minute.

"This noise! Did you hear this noise?"

The door half opened now. Ioannis was trying to see or hear any of these things Hunch was swearing he was seeing and hearing but with zero result.

He knew that those feelings were the results of the hostile vibrations which were going on, all this time.

But was it real what Hunch was sensing or it was all part of his misapprehensions?

A wave of relief flooded over Hunch, he felt like Ioannis believed him but no more than a second later it has been replaced by renewed panic. For him, didn't matter if the only person around believed him or not.

For him now, what mattered was to survive and to do the best to their powers as to bring things in balance.

"Hm . . . Come this way." Ioannis commanded. He walked out on the yard and Hunch followed him with another speech.

"It is high time for us went at the café without another word of denial. It's over and let the house for some minutes unprotected what to do. We will be fast and the fastest we find help the fastest we will come back here. Time to put an end to these jokes. We stayed here doing nothing instead of being out there asking for help." His word sharp as sword, his spirit stronger than any other time. He was convinced for what he had to do. He was heading outside of the yard. He opened the gate and waited for Ioanni to follow.

Now, side by side with the motorbike, was having a brake for his companion to trail.

Ioannis seemed to hesitate.

"Come on man! It will only take us a couple of minutes to run there, please!" his voice took on a pleading note.

But even if Hunch was trying his best on his powers to get Ioanni to follow him, it was unworkable.

His stubbornness however had its reasons.

"Say that we go, what do we tell them? Please help us for our friends gone missing along with our mobiles and car?" with his words he determined that he was going nowhere.

Changed side and he was directing inside the house again while Hunch was waiting side on the motorbike.

"No, wait! Do not go inside please?" he begged him.

"If we lose eye contact maybe we will lose it forever." Hunch said.

Ioannis refuted.

"Come here then!" raged.

Once Hunch saw that he stood there, furious waiting for him, he run. With the psp lighting his face, he asked Ioanni.

"Do you want to stay here? No! Do you want to come with me on the Centre? Forget about material things." Speaking fast, needed a deep breath, and then slowly exhaled.

Yet again Ioannis spat.

"One last look in the house! This time I heard something!"

"You heard? From inside the house?" Hunch asked shocked.

"Yes" but before he finish he cut off by Hunch.

"We need to look after our lives and not the house. Even if there is someone inside, let's go first to ask for HELP!" Hunch on a paradox way demanded but with no appealing.

"We do that, checking on the house and may we go to the villagers. Go first because you have the device with the light." Ioannis guided him.

Hunch showed some signs of denial but he really wanted to leave and find help. There was only one way to do it now and this was to do as Ioannis wanted.

They entered the house for a last time.

***** ***** ***** ***** ***** ***** ***** ***** *****

Ioannis was leading; first they turned right, going at the window with access to the TV-bedroom. Need to check if someone was there, without putting their lives in risk by going inside yet.

With the psp on his hand, was trying to see suspicious movements. Ioannis had also his eyes on it. Nonetheless, nothing seemed out of the ordinary. He nodded him to continue. Hunch was following any instructions Ioannis was giving him.

A sort brake, Ioannis cough. He stopped and made a proposal to Hunch.

"My friend, you can go inside." A commanding but soft note on his voice.

Hunch turned pale. His body deepened in Goosebumps when he heard that. Was he joking or he was really expecting him to enter the house?

"Where do you want me to go?" asked as he had not heard the question.

"In the house. Open the door." Suggesting him to open the thick wooden door of the hall.

"There is no way to enter inside the house! Are you mad?" he roared on him.

Ioannis's face got an aggressive morph. He stood before Hunch, ready to open it by himself.

"Don't go inside!" Hunch blocked him for entering.

"But I heard something. We have to go and check!" Ioannis's voice shrieked. Hunch was not excepting that he, after all these disappearances, would like to do something as reckless as that. He followed until the hall.

He knew, Hunch knew that going deeper into the house was a mistake that should be avoided. In the silence that followed, Ioannis though he heard something coming from the living room: a movement in there. But the sound was too soft for him to be certain, and the atmosphere in the room demanded his absolute fixedness. He needed to check! He wanted to know if he was following Hunch's madness by hearing things which didn't exist.

Carefully, he caught the knob of the door and he opened it. He gazed around and as he saw nothing, he continued.

Their steps were slow, alert; they wanted to cause no noise at all. With Ioanni in front and Hunch as his tail, were moving to the living room.

Ioannis hold back with his hand his friend. He nodded him that he should have a look first and then enter together. He turned his head from the corner of the door and looked around. Nothing seemed to have changed since the last check.

They started back toward the wall. He knew that he had heard something but he didn't want to go there anymore. Maybe he found it useless or maybe he believed that he should forget about it, even if someone was there. For now, they were safe and the truth was that that's what it really mattered.

Outside, there was only a faint glimmer of moonlight. Clouds had covered at the moment half of the moon. But even in the near total darkness they could see the orange light from the electric pole.

Ioannis breathed.

"What shall I tell you now? What do we do?"

"Time to go to the café. No more lies!" hunch's voice dead serious. Only with severity he would be able now to move his friend out of there.

He went on.

"Our friends gone and on times like this one, we have to think logically. We must act like adults. They are missing so what do we do? We go and ask for help." He stated.

"I know, but I am afraid that they will think that we are crazy . . . . I don't want this to happen!" sobbing brokenly.

Hunch hardened his hand.

"Whatever! We have to go and talk to them!"

"And tell them what exactly? That's what you don't get!" Ioannis skepticism was clear in his voice.

Hunch pinned his eyes on him. He was waiting for him to express the doubts he was having.

"Tell them about a GHOST!?" Ioannis shouted with a low tone.

"Of course not!" Hunch knew now why he was objecting all this time.

"We are not going to tell them about a ghost! We are not stupid. The only thing we have to say is that our friends are missing and that's it." He whirled with his words.

Another breath out from Ioanni.

"If we tell them about a ghost, they will not take us seriously. Of course." Hunch said, stretching out each vowel in an exaggerated drawl.

"I . . . I will go and have a look at the first candle again . . ." Ioannis blurted out.

"Apapapa. I am not coming with you in the back yard!" Hunch clarified his position. He used again an old combination of two letters to show his strong objection.

All the old habits which people used to have years ago, Hunch was bringing them on the surface this nigh.

The over reacted action of Hunch, made Ioanni stop.

"If you go there, I give you my word that I will leave you alone and I will go for help, and then, only God will know what is going to happen to you." He threatened him.

"Are you for real?" Ioannis glittered with anger.

"I DO!" Hunch answered back also with anger.

And he left him, started walking at the gate, not wanting to wait in the house any more.

"Stop right there! What are you going to tell them?" Ioannis countered. Hunch made him the favor and he made no more steps but he told him.

"I told you already. Our friends are missing and we need help. I will not mention the words ghosts and we will be fine! Where the hell is Nick?" he asked himself but with an out loud voice to make it clear to Ioanni that he was missing too.

He went out with confidence. He left everything as it was and he didn't care about the house. There was only one purpose on his mind now, ask for help. It was settled.

Watching him like lost, not knowing what to do, Ioannis run after him.

"Close the gate at least!" Hunch voice took on a commanding edge. But no, Ioannis was standing there, biting his lips.

Should follow him was the right choice? They were having a place they were safe until now. Apart from all the noises and shadows they may have seen and heard, the house, or at least, the hall of the house was a good hideout.

Under no account, Ioannis wanted to leave it. He had more than one reasons to stay there and not alone if possible.

"I do not like to repeat myself but if we go there, I do not know what to tell them! How to convince them!" fretted. His speech didn't end there.

"We will tell them that we lost our friends and they will start laughing on us!"

"Do not mention the ghosts then!"

"I never said that I will, but anyhow, they will not believe us!" his note ascended now.

152

Hunch made a snarling face.

"It is a problem which we have to solve. No one will ever believe us." Ioannis spat.

"What time is it?" he asked himself and he walked from the yard to the house, opening the door, entering inside, walking to the TV-bedroom. Above the table there was a clock hanging on the wall. It was the first thing you could see when entering.

He checked.

He went until there only to learn the time. Hunch worried when he saw him going inside without warning and not having another option, he tailed him so as to do not lose him.

"What are you doing? Do you care or not? You are acting like nothing is happening!" he raged at Ioanni.

"I just wanted to know the time." He justified.

Hunch shook his head but he had something to answer him from earlier.

"Whatever . . . I wanted to tell you that this is not something that we have to solve alone, I disagree. Do you believe that you have the required power to crack it?" and without to wait for his answer replied alone.

"You do not, so . . ."

"My opinion it was to stay here from the beginning." Ioannis countered him and he began walking around the house without purpose.

He went from the TV-bedroom to the kitchen and from there to the living room. He was exploring the entire house. He was not looking for something specific, he was just thinking disorganized. His step and his movements reported his feelings. He as well had no idea what his next step should be and this was driving him crazy. He was the type who always had things under control and now, he had to improvise.

He never imagined they would have been trapped, lacking of a second plan. Everything he was doing now, if he wanted to have results, should be very wary and most of all, Hunch should not separate from him. If this would happen, it would be the end.

"It is a GREAT mistake to remain here!" rasping voice screeched from Hunch's own lips.

"For me this is the only option we have right now. I strongly believe that leaving the house will not work out for us." opposed. Still not able to stay in one place, Ioannis was moving from room to room until he ended up in the hall again. Of course Hunch not wanting them to lose eye contact, he was keep following him like a dog.

The hall door shut heavily as Hunch closed it.

"Did you hear that again?" Hunch referred to a sound he heard. Similar to the one he had heard before.

Ioannis was quite, concentrating to hear. Hunch's face grew even tighter. Staying in the house was maybe as fatal as on going outside. To him, the only solution was to go for help even if they had to risk it. After all they had nothing to lose. If staying there was the same as going out, at least, if they were going for help, they may end up find it.

Going outside now, Ioanni's eyes detect all the area they could get. He approached the bar door to the back yard and he closed it. The sound of locking sounded. Hunch came out too and to his surprise, asked him.

"I thought that you had closed it before. Hadn't you?" his voice trailed off.

"I had." Ioannis specified. He looked at Hunch whose face turned out pale again.

"But maybe I didn't. I don't remember. Forget it, anyway it doesn't matter." He told him.

With his mouth opened, gazing to the unknown, Hunch was speechless again and he had the same puzzled face he had before, when he looked like crazy.

Minutes passed deprived of significant events. The main question was still standing. One wanted to go and ask for help to the people of the village and the other, was doing everything on his powers to keep both together there, in the house, where he believed that it was safer.

The conversation wasn't going to an end and the disagreement between the two boys was strong. Eventually, Hunch quitted and he decided to leave Ioanni alone at his house and he to go for help. He had to do something and that was to do not stay there any longer.

As he was leaving, Ioannis made him a last offer.

"Can you please stay here for few more minutes? Give me some time to prepare my words and to think of it and I promise you that we will go together there, at the center. Ok?" he pleaded him, his voice obviously tired from the long night.

Ok." Hunch agreed for last time.

"But after you take your time, we are going and I do not want to listen anything about not going!" Hunch proposed.

"I promise you my friend" replied.

Both outside on the yard, Hunch was waiting for Ioanni to come up with a plan. The good part in all the story was the summer weather. It was night, late at night, and due to the summer heat, they were wearing nothing more than t-shirt on their upper body and they were fine.

Apart from that, the chillness they were feeling was not because of the temperature but because of the thrilling. Even though the night was warm, the sensation of being in danger was making their blood cold, and as cold their blood was, so cold their body sensations were.

***** ***** ***** ***** ***** ***** ***** ***** *****

Approximately, ten minutes had passed from the time Hunch went out on the yard and Ioannis stopped him. His patience was almost on his limit. He was waiting for Ioanni to be mentally and verbally prepared but this was taking him too long.

And then he heard something.

A noise, or better, noises coming from the house!"

"Oh, oh! Do you hear them!?" asked Ioanni with a scared note on his voice.

"What is that?" Ioannis probed him, of course he knew that he didn't know, but he made the question anyway.

Hunch was processing the atmosphere. He didn't want to lose not even the tiniest sound.

"Nick, I am sure he is gone. The shepherd took him already." Ioannis said firmly.

A small tin felt on the ground and Hunch almost lost his life. The cat, the same cat from before, was also there now, jumping around and as a result of its actions, the fall of the tin.

"Go to hell!" Hunch cursed.

Ioannis was ready to say something as he was thinking their next move but Hunch told him to shut up.

"Do not talk and try to listen!" pointed.

Both made silence and now there was indeed a noise surrounding them. Lights appeared, but not from the sky or anywhere else. Those lights where coming from inside the house!

Before they go, they had switched them all off and now this was happening. The house was alive!

"What the!?" Ioannis called and he left everything behind him. He ran furious into the house. He didn't wait for Hunch to tell him not to. He grabbed the knob and before Hunch realizes what was going on, Ioannis had already gone inside the house.

He froze in the spot which he had left him. He was staring at the house. All his body was shaking from fear. Not only he was seeing figures coming from the house but the worse thing was that, he has alone. After all this time he was fighting to do things right and eventually, he ended up alone!

"This cannot be happening." He murmured. He was not able to see what was happening inside because of the thick door on the hall room. But because of these doors glass in the middle, he was able to see figures moving behind it. And that was all. Now he was alone with something so extraordinary happening before his eyes and without knowledge of how to react. Millions of things were passing from his mind. Aliens who had invaded this very house and now they were also inside it. They had captured his friends to make experiments on them and perhaps, he was next.

He also thought that maybe these were figures of thieves. All this, was a long very well made plan to rob them and kill them.

Another explanation his mind was giving, was this of the shepherd. Could it be that the legend was real after all and now, something from another word, a ghost, an alternative oddity, had eaten his friends and it was searching the house for him?

He had now, more than ever to go, to ask people for help. But for some reason, he could not. He passed from its mind to do so but, he was curious. Back in the graveyard, he was intending to go and see the "alien" from close. But he had been stopped by the others. But now, he was all alone, there was no one to stop him. No one to prevent him from going either at the center or the house.

He had to go and ask for help. Now it was his chance. He had to go. He began walking; he knew what he had to do. On no account he would be another one of those stupid victims which dies on the horror movies because they are stubborn. He knew this very well. This was the plan from the start, going and call the police.

So, even if he knew all that, why he was walking to the opposite direction? Why instead of going out of the yard, he was directing straight to the house?

Was he crazy after all? Did he have a death wish?

No, for Hunch was more complicated than this. Whatever was happening now, it was once in someone's life time. Aliens or ghosts, those things don't exist. He had to see them with his own eyes, to touch them to . . . get killed by them. He was having these thoughts too. Maybe this was his last time on the living world. It was a great risk to go inside alone after all these weird and without explanations disappearances, of the mobiles, of the car, of his own friends.

But even though he knew all that, he still had to do so. He had to experience it with his own eyes. All these excitement he was feeling, his blood was boiling, his temperature was rising. He was doing it. He was finally doing it. Aliens, ghost, legend, all these stories was finally the time someone to see if they were, even at their tiniest part, real or not.

He opened the door and he entered the house.

What he heard as first sound entering inside made him immobilize. He did not believe his ears.

***** ***** ***** ***** ***** ***** ***** ***** *****

Was this voice, Ioanni's voice talking with Tony?

And not only, but it was also some other, familiar voices there.

"No, I don't believe it." He heard Ioannis voice saying.

"But this team is the best I believe!" Tony replied.

"They suck . . ." Mr. Snake said, his voice neutral as usually.

"What is that?" Hunch wandered.

"Where are the ghosts? Where are the aliens? Why everyone is here? What is this?" his mind ready to explode.

Hunch was scared. He was feeling that his mental strength will end here. He began feeling dizzy and sick.

He wanted to see something extraordinary, something "alien", but this was not normal neither strange. This was CHAOTIC. If he had seen aliens or ghosts, he would have felt a feeling different than that.

He knew that.

Now, everything was upside down.

"This is what you get when you mess with things where you don't understand? This feeling that feels like you lost your mind?" he though.

Standing now on the door of the living room. Watching his friends sitting, all of them, there, watching the final of Greece got talent as they have said they would.

Tony was the one closer to him. He was sitting on a wooden old chair he had brought from the kitchen table. Nick was sitting on the arm chair, with the controller of the x-box always on his hands. Mr. Snake, right next to Nick on the other arm chair, as they used to be when they were playing the video game, some hours before any of these mystery happens.

Ioannis was standing. He was between Mr. Snake and Void, who was lying on the bed where Mr. Snake were spend the night.

Someone was missing from the picture. Jim was not present in the room at the moment. However, on Hunch's head, this was the last thing to notice.

Nick was having a big smile on his face, watching the show. Last time Hunch saw him, he was upset and he was running for help, and now this. Completely opposite than the time they separated.

But it was not only Nick. It was everyone.

"What is going on?" Hunch though. Still holding the psp on his hand, not able to raise a word. Just observing them.

"I am telling you, this group is going to win the contest, not only because they are good but everyone likes dance.

They are unrivaled." Tony's face illuminated with a smile, talking about the show.

"This chair is uncomfortable." And he moved from the arm chair, to the arm of the arm chair were Nick was sitting.

"I am against them." Mr. Snake sharply added.

"Between the two dancing groups, I also believe that they are the best, but . . . they are not going to take the first place." Ioannis said sparkly.

"You see what they did? That move is AMAZING! "Tony kept saying, making the team even better than already was.

"I would say that the other team was better." Nick said.

"Bullshits." Mr. Snake said eagerly.

Tony gave a glance on Hunch and told him to sit down with them.

"Why are you standing there?" Nick enquired him.

Ioannis began coughing. Mr. Snake at the same time, made a comment about a dancer of the team. Tony forgot about Hunch and he agreed with the comment he made.

The comment was about the dancer's height and everyone agreed that he was looking weird.

"They have chosen a nice song too. And this trick that they just did with the clothes, exchanging them as they dance, they do it all the time." Tony commented again.

"I don't really like this dance." Ioannis pondered, and tired of standing, he sat on Mr. Snake's arm chair's arm.

Tony turned to face the immobilized Hunch once more. Telling him for a second time to sit down with them.

"WHAT THE FUCK IS GOING ON!?" Hunch screamed, the note on his voice clearly scared.

Tony looked at the others.

"Is he alright?" he asked the others.

"Are you alright?" asked Hunch directly this time.

"Grab a chair and sit down with us." Nick suggested him politely.

"Can someone tell Jim to get out of the toilet and come here? He is going to miss all the show." Ioannis raged.

This is what he wanted since they got there, to spend at least one night all together watching this very show. It sounded logical to Hunch that he was shouting, even though he knew that his friend was on men's room. But this happened only for a second.

He knew that something was wrong there.

What had happened? He was absolutely sure that this night had happened. His friends have all gone. He hadn't imagined that or the thing they saw flying on the graveyard, no matter if it was flying or not, he had seen something. Something was seriously going on there. He had a bad feeling about this and he had to react somehow. The only problem was that he could not do anything as he was frozen due to his surprise.

"Will you sit down now or will you stay there all day?" Tony asked him again but Hunch replied only with a tiny smile.

Ioannis stood up, passed next to him and he went to the kitchen.

As he was leaving, he heard Hunch saying that he was seeing ghosts. His tone was asking them indirectly if they knew something about ghosts.

Tony asked him if he was ok and he shouted Ioanni. Before he got what he wanted to tell him, Ioannis cut him off with a question.

"Have you seen my glass? I have one for myself and I don't want anyone to touch it. Is that clear?" someone answered him they hadn't seen it and he didn't continue searching for it as he had just found it.

"Are you a junkie?" Nick questioned Hunch. He indeed was looking like a junkie, staying there, doing nothing just asking silly questions with a covered expression.

Tony on the other hand, was talking with Void about the show.

Ioannis was drinking and finishing his water on the TV-bedroom but he was able to see Hunch who was in front of him in the entrance of the living room, close to the door. He heard him saying.

"How long are you here?" with a concerned voice.

"What do you mean how long? We have watched all the Greece got talent." Mr. Snake replied, his face making an uncharacteristic expression.

"Are you becoming more stupid than you used to be?" asked Hunch.

"He was in the toilet for five minutes but maybe he lost the sense of time. Sometimes it happens to me too. To be there for five minutes and to have the idea that half an hour has past." Ioannis coming back from the kitchen where he had left the glass added.

He passed next to Hunch again and he sat on the arm chair's arm.

The show was playing a mysterious melody and this very moment, Hunch began moving.

He slowly slowly, was directing his hand with his index straight on Tony.

"Are you crazy?" Tony asked him while he could not prevent himself from laughing.

Hunch was also smiling but this smile was different than Tony's. He knew that something was odd. He had to know that they were real. He was afraid they have may ended up being ghosts, or had their brains modified by aliens.

He was ready to touch him but then Tony did a sudden and hostile move. Hunch got scared and stepped back frightened.

Nick and all the others were laughing with Tony's joke.

"Are you crazy Hunch?" Mr. Snake asked him.

"Are you alright?" Nick followed Mr. Snake's question.

"Why are you acting weird?" Tony finally asked him.

"Move your ass and shit down to watch the damn show!" Nick with a satisfied smile commanded.

Tony stood up and tried to catch him. Hunch avoided him and stopped him by making the hand sign for stop.

"Do not touch me!" he declared.

They all looked at him weird.

"Nobody touches me! Something is going on here! This is not a joke!" his voice having an unusual for his character commanding tone.

"What the . . ." Tony stammered, looking at him weird.

Hunch was trying to figure out what could possible had happened. Should he trust them at this point or not? Were these people his friends?

"Hunch, do not say that we have no right to make fun on you!" Nick said.

"He is right!" Ioannis agreed with Nick.

"You slept for five minutes and you lost your mind?" Tony said with query. Ioannis stood up, walked next to them, leaving the room.

"Ioanni, wait!" Hunch shouted on him. There was something which Hunch wanted to know, he wanted to ask him a certain thing. After all, Ioannis was the only one who had stayed with him the entire time. He had only missed him for five minutes. Was it possible that between these fine minutes, something changed him?

Or he was crazy after all?

"I need to ask you something!" pleaded him.

But Ioannis did not answer, on the contrary, he ignored him and Void followed him. They started talking about a joke they had said earlier, while Hunch was sleeping.

When Hunch saw that he was not responding, he made another question. He noticed this time, that Jim was missing for a long time. Even for Jim, being in the toilet for so long, something was definitely odd.

"Where is Jim?" he asked with a loud voice. His purpose was not someone to answer him that he was in the toilet but to make them think that there were blank spots from the night.

He could not have been the only one who knew the truth. You can tell when you are dreaming and when not. He was certain that he wasn't! So he had to make questions to get some answers.

There was a brake on the show and everyone left their seats. Tony went to drink some water and Nick was wandering around stretching. Even though Hunch was asking them things about this night, no one seemed to worry. They were telling him to calm down and that he was acting weird. He was trying to do not mention ghosts at this point or their disappearances, at least he was not that stupid, but he was making simple questions as, who had appeared before the dancing team on the show or why they were wearing their shoes.

This was a very good question he made.

He knew that they were watching the show on the TV-bed room and not at the living room. He also remembered that they were not wearing shoes.

Actually only Ioannis and Void were wearing shoes at the moment but he had to know why.

"Ioanni, why are you wearing your shoes inside the house?" He asked him as he was still talking with Void, before the show starts again.

Ioannis exchanged looks with Void.

"And you Void, why?" Hunch repeated the question.

"Because we went out dumbass! Isn't it obvious?" Ioannis scold him.

"And why you went out!?" He asked them, his temper was rising.

"What the fuck do you want?" Ioannis raged.

164

"Are you ok Hunch?" Void tried to see what was wrong with him.

"Forget it . . ." Hunch mumbled.

The TV played the opening song, and everyone sat again down.

They did not sit in the seats they were seating before. They just sat random, anywhere they found. Ioannis was the only one who didn't follow. He was looking outside the long window of the entrance hall.

"I have an idea!" he suddenly screamed. He went on the living room and stood next to Hunch. He was not sitting anywhere, just standing. He obviously didn't have the courage to sit.

"Why don't we go out, to explore the village? And to make fun of this legend my father told us about! The shepherd!" he proposed joyfully.

Hunch looked at him and he turned pale.

"Why did he say that?" He thought.

"Wait, not now. Let's watch the show first and then." Tony told him, his voice calm.

"Now?" Nick energetically asked. It seemed like he wanted to go out.

"Tony is right. Let's see who is going to win this thing and then we go for ghost hunting!" Ioannis pointed.

Mr. Snake went close to Ioanni. He whispered him on the ear.

"Come with me for a second. I need to speak to you."

"For your girlfriend, isn't it?"

Mr. Snake nodded.

"I am coming." They gone in the kitchen were they also closed the door to talk in private.

No more than two minutes later, the door opened and they walked out. Ioannis was telling Mr. Snake what he had to do in a relationship in order to do not blow it as he did. The room was enriched with life. They were having lots of fun, talking, watching the show, laughing, enjoying the moment. Everyone than Hunch.

"Did you make all this? Was it a prank?" He asked and he started having suspicions on that matter.

They looked at him and they began laughing.

"What are you talking about man?" Mr. Snake said first. Then Tony followed.

"You are the only person that . . ." but didn't manage to finish as Hunch cut him off.

"I want to know what is going on. If this is not a prank, then I am crazy!" he yelled out again.

"First of all, why do you have my psp on your hand?" Ioannis said and took it from its hand. Everyone laughed with it. Even Hunch lost it for a minute and showed a smile.

This was only at the minute.

He refocused again and asked loudly.

"Am I seeing ghosts?" his eyes flaming over terror.

Jim came this moment out of the toilet and joint them in the living room.

"I had . . . . A hard time let's say." He seemed kind of proud that he had stayed in the toilet for so long. The laughs filled all the room once more. The air was entertaining and Hunch had to do something. He was feeling dizzy and confused. The worst of all was that he was sure he had this night. If aliens or ghosts had done something to them, they would not remember. He was conflicted.

A titan class on his head for the truth.

"You have lost the last three appearances boy." Nick told Jim cheerily.

"We agreed to go out and look for the legend of the shepherd. Are you coming?" Ioannis asked him.

"Yes sure. Around twelve right?" Jim modestly named.

Ioannis nodded. Twelve was the right time to go for ghost hunting.

"My mother called me. Shit, I had in on silent mode." Void panicked said as he was looking on his mobile screen.

"Is it late to call her back?' Tony tried to calm him.

"It is eleven and a half. My mother sleeps early. Anyway, I hope that she is not going to scold me tomorrow that I didn't answer." Void's voice sounded soother.

Hunch was still examining them. He didn't know whether to trust them or not.

"Ghost hunting! I am looking forward to it!" Ioannis grinned triumphantly.

"If we go far, shall we take the car? I am bored to walk to be honest." Nick condensed to Ioanni.

"The car . . . Why not? We will see, ok?"

Hunch made an exceptional question that could have saved him. He unzipped the small bag which he had with him the entire time on his waist and after he searched inside, he inquired.

"Where is my mobile?" his tone extremely sharp, waiting for the answer. Now he would have a chance to catch them. They had lost the mobiles long before the disappearances. What would they answer him now?

"I think is there, where you left it to charge. If I am not mistaking." Ioannis told him.

He tried to remember where it was the charger socked but Tony interrupted his thoughts.

"You slept five minutes and you are acting like . . . I don't know what. Are you that stupid?"

"You want to tell me that I was sleeping?" Hunch said furiously.

"If you weren't sleeping, then tell me what did you watch? Before the dancers who was it? And before them who else?" Tony put him on the corner.

Of course and he had no idea who was before the dancers since he had never watched the show. Could it be that he was really sleeping?

"I have any reason to make fun on you now." Nick declared. Not that he was not already making fun of him, but he was always looking up for a new excuse.

"Ok . . . I will not talk again." Frustrated announced and left the room.

"Can I advise you something?" Nick asked him from his position but Hunch didn't respond. He was already out of the room.

"Yes, it is all as you say. You are right, ghosts exist!" Tony said ironically. Whereas Tony and Nick were mocking him, Jim went after him. He looked ridiculous, wearing a t-shirt on the colors of the army and a blue short pant. He tried to reason him but Hunch pushed him away. Jim returned to the living room, staying with the others, watching the winner of the show.

"Am I crazy? Did I really sleep and I thought that this was real? It looked real. It can't be that I was sleeping and I dreamed all that . . . If it is not a prank then, a well-made prank, then they don't know what happened." Inside his head, those thoughts were spinning like a roller coaster.

The mobiles . . . he found his mobile in the charging socket as they told him. But they have lost them long before the appearance of the supernatural phenomena. Then why he doubted? Was this part of the prank or he just dreamed everything? The phone was working properly and he checked, not once but twice. The car was also there. He should have heard the noise if they were driving it back to the house. Being the house next to the road, gives this privilege of hearing anything.

He had to make a last try.

Entering for one more time in the living room. They were ready to leave and go for ghost hunting as they were planning. The show was over but so as Hunch's patience. He hide his sameness and he asked with clear and loud voice so everyone in this room, including Nick and Void who were talking loudly with each other, to hear him.

"Was this all a well-made prank!?" the words came out of his mouth impatiently. He was desperate to know the truth. He was screaming for it, he needed, no, he had to know what had happened.

He managed to collect all the eyes on him. They all turned their heads, staring at him with empty eyes. Then as Hunch was waiting for the answer which will purified him, some started to laugh. Some others shook their heads as a sign of pity.

This night, Hunch didn't sleep.

They told him that while he was sleeping at the show, he was mumbling the following words, sweating.

"The car . . . Where is the car?"

All made sense now. He was in no movie. Nothing ever happened. It was all part of his imagination and nothing more. He was sleeping all this time and he believed that the dream that he had dreamed about was true. The thought of going at a doctor didn't seem bad at this point.

But still . . . . something was weird. Something he didn't like. Some parts in the story they told him were wrong.

In the end, was it a dream or not?

One thing is certain.

Months later, Hunch was saying to people that once he had seen a dream which he had believed it was the reality . . .